Edward is grateful he's not the family company's CEO and that he doesn't have to make the decisions his brother Henry has to make. He supports Henry, of course, but signing contracts with a fire wielder while they're earth wielders could be dangerous, with Purity threatening them.

Bay is happy working for Dakota, even though he's kind of jealous of his best friend for finding love. He's more than happy to help when the Long brothers, who Dakota's mate is working with now, are threatened. Bay is assigned as a bodyguard to Edward, who's charming and sweet—and it turns out, also Bay's mate.

But Purity is still a threat, especially after it attacks. Faking Henry's death might have been a good idea, but it also could be putting Edward's life in danger, and Bay isn't sure he can stand up to Purity, not on his own, not when Purity has someone working for them on the inside.

Earth and Water
Copyright © 2020 Catherine Lievens
ISBN: 978-1-4874-2969-0
Cover art by Angela Waters

Published by eXtasy Books Inc or
Devine Destinies, an imprint of eXtasy Books Inc

Look for us online at:
www.eXtasybooks.com or www.devinedestinies.com

Earth and Water
Elemental Unions Book 2

By

Catherine Lievens

CHAPTER ONE

Edward didn't want to go to the meeting. He looked at his reflection in the mirror and straightened his tie for what felt like the tenth time.

Why did he have to go, anyway? *Right.* It was because he'd already met Benedict and Dakota while Henry hadn't.

His bedroom door slammed open, and Henry stepped in, still buttoning his shirt. Edward glared at him through the mirror before focusing on his own reflection again.

"You look pretty, don't worry," Henry said.

Edward had to turn around so his glare would have a better effect. His tie was fine, anyway. He leaned against the dresser and crossed his arms over his chest, looking at his brother. "Why are you here?"

"I wanted to talk to you before the meeting."

Edward sighed. "I should never have given you a key. And why are you buttoning your shirt?" Edward squinted. "Wait. Is that *my* shirt?"

Henry gave Edward a remorseless grin. "I spilled coffee on mine. Sorry."

"Why were you even having coffee in my kitchen? Why are you in my apartment? I need you to give me back my key."

Henry shook his head. "No way. I have to be able to come in if something happens to you. I don't want you to end up dead in here and not be found for weeks."

Edward needed strength to deal with his brother, and he wasn't sure he had enough. "What did you want to talk about?"

1

Henry finished buttoning the shirt. "How are they? Dakota and Benedict, I mean. You said they're dating, right?"

"Dakota is Benedict's boyfriend, yes." It should have been obvious to Edward as soon as he'd stepped into the office.

He hadn't wanted to ask who Dakota was in the beginning, because it wasn't his business and because he was walking on eggshells around Benedict. Everyone was. The man was ambitious, and he was trying to do a good thing, but Edward hadn't known if he could trust him, and he still didn't, not entirely. He wanted to, but he wasn't stupid. No matter what Benedict and Dakota said, they might be lying, and Edward couldn't afford to believe them entirely.

"And they wield different elements," Henry continued.

"I didn't ask them to prove it to me, but they said they do. We know Benedict wields fire, while Dakota apparently wields earth."

Henry wrinkled his nose. "It's weird, isn't it? That they're together even though their elements are different. How did they even meet? Elements don't mix."

Edward shouldn't have been amused, but he was. "You're sheltered. The only people you know are the ones who share our element or humans. Not everyone is like you, though."

Henry glared. "I'm not sheltered."

"You are. Everyone in the company either wields the earth element or is human. And I know why." They both did. It wasn't their fault. Even if they tried hiring a diverse pool of employees, only earth wielders applied. It was how things went, but maybe now, it would change. "But we can change it. We can change the world as we know it."

Henry sucked in a breath. "Sometimes, I wonder if it's the best thing to do."

Edward wanted to reassure him, but he wasn't sure he could. He wasn't even sure they should be doing this, no matter how right it was. "We're doing the right thing."

Henry wrinkled his nose. "Some people don't believe that."

"And does what they believe matter? You're doing this for the right reasons. Hell, even if they were the wrong reasons, it would still be the right thing to do."

Because Edward truly believed the elements were meant to mix. Why would some of them find their mates in other elements if that wasn't the case? Of course, not a lot of people did these days, but that was because they didn't give themselves a chance, not because it wasn't possible.

"We still have to trust Benedict Hunt if we're going to do this, and I don't know if I do. Why is he doing this? Is it really because he believes in it the way we do?"

Edward had heard Benedict had been attacked and that he'd killed people. He didn't know if that was true or not, but even if Benedict *had* killed his attackers, Edward didn't blame him. He'd had to defend himself. If Edward had been in Benedict's place, he would have killed the person who'd attacked him, too.

Or maybe not. He probably would have been killed, but then, he was who he was, while Benedict was a strong man who had the support of many people. Not that Edward didn't. Henry would always be there for him, and so would their mom, even though she was always busy.

But they were the only ones. Edward didn't like people, and he didn't do relationships, for reasons that were out of his control. Maybe it was better that way, but he couldn't help how lonely he felt some days.

He shook his head, pushing the thoughts away. "I don't know for sure. Benedict seems to be a good and serious man, and from the conversation we had, I truly think he believes in what he's doing. It's business, of course, but it was obvious to me that he was aiming at something more."

"Do you know why? It can't just be because of his

boyfriend."

Edward took a minute to think. He couldn't explain Benedict and Dakota's relationship to his brother, because he didn't know anything about it. "Well, Dakota cares about him. He came to talk to me after the meeting was over, and I'm pretty sure he loves Benedict. I didn't ask him, of course, but they're a real couple. I have no doubt about that. So maybe this *is* why Benedict is doing this, or maybe not. He started this a while ago, and the deal he signs with you won't be the first one. But even if he's doing this because of his boyfriend, is it a bad reason? He and Dakota want to be together, and they want to be happy. The fact that they wield different elements means they're a target for Purity, and that can't be easy."

Henry scowled. "Purity. I want to get my hands on them and make sure they don't hurt anyone."

"Don't we all?" Purity was a danger to the delicate balance between the different elements, and Edward could only imagine what would happen if they broke that balance.

He didn't want to imagine it. He didn't want to think about what would happen if they continued on the path they were following. Death, no doubt, and a lot of it. Edward didn't understand why Purity thought the various elements needed to stay away from each other so badly that they were ready to kill to make it happen, and he didn't think he would even if they explained. Some people just didn't make sense.

But they were dangerous, and Edward and Henry needed to be careful, as careful as Benedict was being. Edward didn't know what would happen during the meeting, but they needed to talk to Benedict about this, since he seemed to have more information than they did about Purity.

Hopefully, he would answer their questions. They needed him to. They couldn't be in the dark, not when it came to this business relationship, or when it came to the target Purity would put on them, too, as soon as this became public knowledge.

"Eddie?"

Henry's voice cut through Edward's thought. "Yes?"

"It'll be okay, you know."

Edward blinked. "What?"

"I know you're worried, but I promise that if this is too dangerous, I'll step out."

"This deal is important." And not just because of how it would help their business. Even though it was dangerous, Edward wanted the elements to be able to mix and do what they wanted. He might be afraid, but he was ready to face that fear and Purity—for now. Nothing bad had happened to him or his brother yet, and he couldn't be sure he'd still feel the same if it did.

"It is, yeah," Henry continued. "But you're more important. I won't put your safety at risk, or mine, no matter how much I think Hunt is right. I want this to go well, but if we have to bow out, then I'll do just that."

"Don't worry about me, Henry. I'll be fine." Edward wasn't the face of their company. Henry was, and if something happened, if Purity came after them, he would be the one to get hurt, not Edward.

Bay didn't understand why Dakota was so nervous. "It's not like you're going on a first date," he pointed out.

Dakota glared at him, and Bay rolled onto his stomach. He was spread out on Dakota's bed, and he was trying very hard not to think about what Dakota and Benedict got up to in it.

"Of course I'm nervous. This could mean a lot for Benedict's company."

"But he's rich. Even if this deal doesn't go through, it's not like he's going to become poor or anything."

Dakota's glare deepened, and Bay knew he'd said the wrong thing. "We're not thinking about money here, Bay. We're talking about reuniting the elements, about making life easier both for Benedict and me and Quillan and Rhea. But you wouldn't understand. When was the last time you had a long-term relationship?"

Bay glared at him. "My relationships don't have anything to do with this." But he understood what Dakota was saying. The critical part of this deal wasn't the money, but rather, showing the rest of the element wielders that different elements *could* work together.

Bay had always known that was the case, of course. Dakota wielded earth, while Bay wielded water, yet they were best friends. They'd worked together for years and had been friends even longer, and nothing would ever change that, especially not what kind of element they wielded. That detail didn't change who they were, or the fact that they were human beings who had friendships and fell in love with people who didn't wield their elements.

He knew teasing Dakota and making him talk would help him relax, though, so he continued,

"Well, I can't wait to see what happens," he said. "Benedict is a genius at what he does. I don't know why you're so worried. He'll have them eating out of his hand in seconds."

Dakota relaxed, his shoulders slumping a bit. "I'm still not sure we need everyone there," he said.

Bay wouldn't compromise on that, though. "Even if you don't need us, it can't be a bad thing to have protection." Especially after that video had gone live a few weeks ago.

Purity puzzled Bay. He understood what they were saying, but from what Dakota had explained about the attack against him and Benedict, Purity used different element wielders. Why did they do that? They wanted the elements to work separately and not to have any kind of contact, yet when they'd attacked Benedict and Dakota, the attackers had belonged to all four elements. Bay knew why, of course. That way, they'd thought they would manage to get to Benedict without a problem. Benedict was known because he was a successful CEO, not because he was a fighter, and Bay knew Dakota had been impressed by how well he'd held his own.

So in a way, it made sense that Purity had sent all four elements, but why were they working together in Purity in the first place if Purity thought they shouldn't? Bay had been trying to solve that question since it had happened, without result. He didn't think he'd solve it unless he could ask questions to some of the Purity members, and he doubted that would ever be possible. If he ever stumbled onto one of those, he'd kick their ass, not ask them questions.

Dakota turned to face Bay again. "You think Purity will try to stop us?"

"Well, I don't think they'll be able to get into the building." Bay would make sure they didn't. Even though Dakota was the boss, he would be in that meeting, and that meant he needed to be protected just like Benedict. He wouldn't be able to focus on that protection, but Bay would. That was why he was Dakota's second, and he intended to make Dakota proud of him. Dakota would no doubt focus his attention on Benedict, no matter what, so Bay would keep his attention on everything else.

"You need to be ready," Dakota said. "I don't want you or anyone else to get hurt because of this meeting."

"We'll be fine. You need to focus on what's going on in that office and on your mate. Let me and the others worry about what's going on outside and make sure nothing happens."

Dakota shook his head. "I want you and Alcott in the office with us, just in case."

Bay set up and frowned. "Just in case? What's going on? And don't say nothing, because I know you, and you'll be lying if those words come out of your mouth."

Dakota wrinkled his nose. "Nothing is happening. I promise. It's not a lie. And I do sort of trust Edward and his brother, even though I've never met Henry. Everything I found out about the brothers points to them being serious about the deal and the reason they want to seal it. Still, I don't know them personally. They're not friends, and I don't know if I can trust them. It's also dangerous, especially with the video from Purity. I don't want anything to happen, and I'd feel better if I knew Benedict has close protection."

"He'll have you. You provide better protection than anyone else." Except when he was distracted by Benedict's ass, but Bay wasn't about to point that out.

"Yeah, but if something happens, I'll be distracted. I'll be frantic about Benedict, and I want to make sure that both of us are safe. Look, you can send someone else if you're not feeling up to sitting in on the meeting, but I'd rather have you."

"That's fine with me. I was just making sure it was the best thing." Honestly, Bay felt better knowing he would be right there. He couldn't deny he was nervous about the meeting.

It wasn't just Purity, although that was the biggest part of it. Bay still couldn't figure them out, but what they wanted was obvious. He was pretty sure that whoever was behind them wanted the elements to be separated so they would be weaker, and once they were, Purity would take over. Having the elements united the way they'd been moving toward recently wouldn't work well for Purity. It would probably ruin their business, whoever they were.

That was why Bay had a list of people who might be behind Purity, mostly people who ran in the same circles as Benedict, albeit made of different elements. The problem was that he had no idea how to find out who the culprit was, no matter how many times he stared at his list.

"We'll be there," he confirmed. He wanted to be at the

meeting because he was curious. He and Dakota had always known that different elements could work together, but most people tended to ignore that and be opposed to it. Benedict was different, but it seemed that Edward and Henry might be, too. Bay wanted to meet them.

"Good." A knock on the door made both Bay and Dakota turn.

It opened, and Benedict stuck his head in. "Almost ready?" He flashed a smile to Dakota, then noticed Bay, too, and gave him a quick smile before turning his attention back to his mate.

Dakota beamed at him as if he hadn't seen him just an hour ago. "Almost. Which tie do you think would be better?" he asked, lifting two of them.

Bay had watched Dakota go back and forth between them, and he was grateful Benedict would take the choice out of Dakota's hands.

Benedict stepped in, shaking his head. "You don't have to wear a tie if you don't want to. You're not sitting in on the meeting. I am."

"Maybe, but they know I'm your boyfriend. They expect me to be there."

"So? You walked around my office in jeans and a t-shirt for weeks. Why do you suddenly want to wear a suit?"

Dakota's cheeks flushed, and Bay had to look away when Benedict stepped behind him with one of the ties.

This was what he wanted. He'd never been jealous of Dakota. His best friend deserved everything he was getting, including Benedict—especially him. They were in love, and it was a good thing.

But Bay was jealous now. Dakota hadn't even wanted to meet his mate, yet he had. Why hadn't Bay, who *wanted* to meet them? He didn't have an answer to that. Of course, he might already have met his mate and didn't know about it.

Realizing who your mate was could be such a complicated thing that sometimes, it felt like Bay would never find his.

He couldn't lose faith, though. If Dakota had found Benedict and Quillan had found Rhea, then Bay could find his own mate eventually. In the meantime, he needed to focus on keeping his people safe, and that included Dakota and Benedict.

He peeked at the couple again, then turned his head toward the wall. They weren't done yet. Benedict was tying the tie around Dakota's neck, and they were softly talking.

Then they kissed, and the sound made Bay's heart hurt. Yes, he could wait. He could focus on protecting his family and making sure that once he found his mate, he would be able to be with them and to focus on them. That didn't mean waiting didn't hurt, though. Bay wanted what Dakota and Benedict had. He didn't know if he would ever have it, but he wasn't about to lose hope. He was still young, and as Dakota and Benedict had shown, he could meet his mate at any moment, and it could be anyone.

He was impatient, but then, who wouldn't be when it came to getting their happily ever after?

Edward bounced his knee as the elevator went up. He didn't want to be here, but he knew his brother needed him. That was why Henry had sent him to meet Benedict first. He'd wanted to know what Benedict was like and whether he was serious about making a deal between their two businesses. Still, it didn't mean that Edward was comfortable with this. He wasn't the one who had this kind of meeting. He was the one who worked behind the scenes, making sure everything was the way it should be so that Henry could sweep in and sign deals and do whatever else he did.

There was a reason Henry was the one who'd inherited the

business from their father. Henry had been surprised and appalled in the beginning, but Edward and their father had made the decision together. Edward had never wanted to be in Henry's place. He'd never wanted to be the CEO, or to have any kind of power. He enjoyed working for Henry, even though they were brothers, or maybe because of it. He liked making sure that Henry's life was as easy as it could be.

"Stop bouncing your knee," Henry murmured without looking at Edward.

Edward stopped instantly. "Sorry."

"Don't worry about it. You can't show people you're nervous, though. They'll take advantage of it."

Edward didn't think Benedict would, even though he barely knew him, but he nodded anyway. "This is why I'm not the one who makes deals," he murmured.

"You could if you wanted to, but we've already talked about it, and I know what you think. I won't push."

Edward was relieved. He was even more relieved when the elevator pinged and the doors slid open. He stepped out and looked around, searching for Benedict's secretary. He knew she would be the one to greet them, and he smiled at her when she came closer. He tried to remember her name, but he couldn't, so he limited himself to holding his hand out to greet her.

"Good morning," he said.

She smiled back. "Mr. Hunt is waiting for you. If you want to follow me?"

Amanda. That was her name. Edward nodded at her. "Lead the way, Amanda. We'll be right behind you."

Her smile widened, as if the fact that he'd remembered her name was a good thing. She turned around, and Edward fell into step with her.

He hoped this meeting would go well, and not just because he'd liked Benedict and Dakota when he'd met them. He knew the odds weren't in their favor, and not merely because of Purity. He doubted Purity would be able to get inside of the building, but he couldn't be sure, and he was afraid, both for himself and for his brother.

But something needed to be done. The elements needed to get closer again. There weren't a lot of them left, although it was hard to tell, since they didn't mix. Edward was sure of it, though, just like he was sure that if they didn't start to mix, they might disappear entirely. It would be a huge loss, even though humans weren't even aware of their existence.

And of course, Edward wanted to make their father proud, even though he wasn't with them anymore. He wasn't sure this was the best way to do it. He wasn't even sure what his father would think about reuniting the elements the way they'd been before the war. Edward felt that they needed to do it, though. He wasn't a businessman like his brother. He didn't have any kind of power. He didn't *want* any kind of power. But maybe, in this, he could help.

Amanda stopped in front of the door of Benedict's office and knocked. When he called out to her to enter, she opened the door and stepped aside. "Mr. Hunt? Edward and Henry Long are here."

"Let them in," Benedict answered.

Edward nodded at Amanda as he walked into the office. He wasn't surprised to see that Benedict was behind his desk and that his boyfriend was on the other side of it, but he *was* surprised to see the other two men in the office. He hadn't expected them, but maybe he should have. They all knew how dangerous this meeting could become if Purity found out about it.

Benedict rose to his feet, already smiling. "Edward. It's a pleasure to see you again," he said, holding his hand out as he walked around the desk.

Edward moved toward him, taking his hand and shaking

it. "Same." He stepped aside to introduce Henry. "And this is my brother, Henry. He's the one you'll be meeting with. I'm just here for moral support."

Benedict laughed. "It's the same reason I have Dakota with me. It's a pleasure to meet you, Henry. I can call you Henry, right?"

Henry nodded. He was already smiling, and Edward knew he liked Benedict.

Edward cleared his throat and gestured toward the sitting area at the back of the room. "I'll be waiting back there."

Benedict nodded. "As you can see, there are two men here with us today. They're bodyguards, and they work for Dakota. We wanted to be sure nothing would happen during this meeting," he explained. "Alcott is next to the door, while the man in the sitting area is Bay."

Edward gave both of them a smile before turning back to Benedict and Henry. "I'll leave you to your work."

He was relieved that he could step away, but surprised when he sat in one of the armchairs and Bay came closer.

"I'm Bay," he said.

"I'm Edward. Shouldn't you be focused on the meeting?"

"Why should I? It's none of my business."

Edward blinked. "You're a bodyguard. You're supposed to keep your eyes on your clients."

"And right now, you're my client. Benedict will be fine. Dakota isn't looking away from him even for one second. Alcott is focusing on the door, so I don't have to do that, either. You're my only focus until the meeting ends. So, do you want anything to drink? I'm not sure what I can find, but I do know there's coffee and water."

Edward didn't know what to say to that. He wasn't sure what to think about being Bay's only focus. The thought made him wiggle in his seat, and he forced himself to stop and smile blandly at Bay. "Water is fine, thank you."

Bay's smile was more natural. "I'll grab it for you. Wait here."

"I'm not going anywhere unless Edward is, too. Don't worry."

He watched Bay as he walked away. He didn't go far, just off the sitting area, and he opened the closet. Since Edward could only see the back of him, he focused on that, even though he could feel his cheeks heat.

He didn't feel any kind of sexual desire for Bay — or for anyone — but he couldn't deny the man was sexy as hell. He seemed to have a great body under his clothes, and while Edward didn't want to explore it, he wouldn't have minded seeing it. He liked looking at pretty things, and Bay was more than a little pretty.

He pushed those thoughts away. He couldn't afford to think of them. He needed to focus on the meeting and what would come out of it.

He turned toward Henry, but his brother wasn't even looking at him. He was deep in conversation with Benedict, nodding at something Benedict was saying, gesturing when he answered. Edward knew that if he wanted, he could go up to them and become part of their conversation, but why should he? He wasn't part of that world. He probably wouldn't understand half of what they were saying.

His father had tried several times to teach Edward how to step into his shoes when he died or decided to retire. He'd wanted Henry and Edward to work together, but Edward had never managed to learn. His brain couldn't make sense of the numbers and everything that was necessary to lead the family business, and he'd been more than happy to let Henry take that place. He still was. They worked together, even though they didn't have the same kind of responsibilities.

But he was worried. The deal would put Henry in front of Purity, and it would make a target out of him more than

Edward. Edward didn't like it. He knew that talking to Henry about it wouldn't change anything, though. Henry was stubborn, and he thought he was doing the right thing. Edward thought so, too, which was why he wouldn't try to stop his brother.

"Here you go," Bay said. He handed Edward a bottle of water, and Edward took it.

"Thank you."

Bay's smile was sweet. He sat in the armchair next to Edward, as if to keep him company. "Don't worry about it."

Edward had to look away so he wouldn't get caught staring.

He had no idea why he was thinking about that kind of thing when it came to Bay. He wasn't attracted to him, not in the sense most people were attracted to other people, but he couldn't deny he was interested.

Bay seemed like an interesting kind of person. Edward didn't know him, so of course, he could be wrong, but he found himself wanting to ask questions, like for example, why he'd become a bodyguard or how working with Dakota was.

He didn't.

He stayed quiet, but he couldn't ignore Bay's presence next to him, not even when he wasn't looking at him. He didn't know why, and he wasn't sure he wanted to find out. What he was sure of was that he was interested in Bay more than he'd been in anyone in a long time, and he wasn't quite sure what to do with that.

Even though Bay was talking to Edward, he was still aware of everything that was happening in the room, so he didn't feel too guilty about the fact that he was intrigued by Edward.

He didn't like the fact that Edward seemed kind of

spooked, though. He kept looking at the door and windows as if he expected someone to barge in and try to kill them. Bay doubted anything like that would happen, and he wanted Edward to relax. Besides, Dakota had told him that while he wanted him and Alcott to be there during the meeting, he didn't actually expect anything to happen. The entire building was under control, and they would know if anyone tried to come anywhere near it with bad intentions.

"So, why are you not involved in the meeting?" he asked.

Edward frowned at him. "Because I'm not the owner of the company."

"But you're his brother."

"And?"

"Well, why aren't you one of the owners? It would make sense if you were."

Edward's frown deepened. "Shouldn't you be focusing on keeping Henry safe? I know you said you were supposed to stick with me, but still. He and Benedict are the important ones here."

Bay couldn't help but smile. "Don't worry. I know exactly where everyone is in the room, and I'll protect you and your brother if something happens. But there are three of us and three of you. I'm sure Alcott will be there for your brother if someone attacks him. That's why I'm sticking with you."

To Bay's dismay, Edward's expression changed to wariness. "You think someone is going to attack us?"

"I *know* nothing like that will happen." He leaned even closer so he wouldn't disturb the meeting. "You know Dakota owns a private security company, right?"

"I do."

Of course he did. He and his brother would have no doubt looked into Dakota and Benedict, and Benedict had mentioned that Alcott and Bay worked for Dakota. "Well, Dakota is taking advantage of that. The entire building is protected.

We have people checking who walks in and out and checking all the floors to make sure nothing happens. The fact that Alcott and I are here isn't actually for security, not entirely anyway. I think Dakota wanted to make sure you and your brother were relaxed and that having another two people here who were from different elements would help with that."

Edward cocked his head and looked at Dakota. "He thought of everything, didn't he?"

"That's Dakota for you. He's a great business owner, and I don't want you to be worried. I promise. We have everything in hand."

Bay didn't expect Edward to trust him or believe him, so he was surprised when Edward slowly nodded. "Thank you. You said you wield a different element from Dakota and Benedict?"

"I'm a water wielder." Bay already knew Edward and Henry were earth wielders, and Alcott wielded air. "All four elements are represented today."

Edward's gaze moved to Alcott, and Bay had to restrain himself from saying anything about it. He didn't know what it was about Edward, but he wanted Edward's attention on him, not on Alcott.

"So he wields air?" Edward asked.

"He does. If you ask me, I think water and earth are perfect together, though."

Edward's focus turned back to Bay. His eyes were wider, as if he couldn't quite believe what Bay had just said.

Bay couldn't believe it himself.

"I'm sorry?"

Bay shook his head. "Forget it." He needed to shift Edward's focus onto something that wasn't what he'd said. He wanted to distract Edward before he could ask more questions Bay didn't know how to answer. "It's like nothing else exists apart from their conversation," he said, tilting his chin toward Benedict and Henry so Edward would know what he was talking about.

Edward smiled. "My brother is always like this. He's a good business owner."

"So is Benedict."

"You would think, that since you're his friend."

Bay startled in surprise. "Actually, *Dakota* is my friend, not Benedict."

"Since they're together, they have to both be your friends, don't they?"

Bay shrugged. "I don't know Benedict well enough to be his friend, but I do like him. He's good for Dakota."

And Bay thought Edward would be good for him, although he wasn't about to say *that* out loud.

Edward nodded and looked back at the meeting. He was more relaxed now, and Bay was relieved and happy that he'd been able to do that for him.

Edward was cute, and he looked sweet. Bay wasn't sure what that meant, but he was sure of one thing—Edward was way out of his league.

There was no denying that, and Bay wasn't about to. Even though Edward wasn't a rich business owner, he was still Henry Long's brother. He worked with Henry, and from what Dakota had managed to find—and it had been difficult, because Edward didn't seem to enjoy the spotlight and stayed behind the scenes—Edward had been vital for several of the deals his brother had signed. From what Bay understood, he went first, meeting with people and deciding whether or not it would be worth his brother's time to talk to them. Bay supposed they were lucky he'd liked Benedict enough to agree to this second meeting.

Bay wouldn't have met him otherwise.

Bay needed to stop dreaming. He didn't even know why he was thinking that way. He didn't know Edward, no matter how many times he'd read the notes Dakota had taken on him. Edward was a good man, and Bay was convinced of that. That didn't mean there could be anything between them, though. As far as he knew, Edward didn't have anyone in his life, but the fact that Dakota hadn't found anything could simply mean Edward was intensely private. It wouldn't be a bad thing, especially with Purity creating problems.

Or maybe Edward was single. Did it matter that Bay didn't know him yet? Wasn't that how every relationship started? Dakota and Benedict hadn't known each other when they'd first met, either, and they hadn't fallen in love at first sight. They'd worked together for a while, and Bay knew Dakota had started to fall in love with his mate even before the attack and the revelation that they were mates. Couldn't the same thing happen between Bay and Edward?

Edward was good looking. He was taller than Bay, although that wasn't hard, since Bay was only five foot eleven. He was thin, but his body looked soft, and Bay wanted to find out if that was the case. He wanted to get to know Edward.

They belonged to two different social circles, though. Once the meeting was over, Bay doubted they'd ever see each other again unless Edward or Henry hired him for their personal security, and that would mean that Edward was even more out of reach. Bay didn't sleep with clients, and he didn't fall in love with them.

Something told him his heart would make an exception for Edward, though, and he had no clue how to deal with this and all the other things he was feeling. He was confused.

Now wasn't the moment to talk to Edward and maybe ask him if he wanted to speak to Bay again, but that didn't mean there would never be a good moment. Bay didn't think he could let go of this, not when Edward could be his mate. Hell, Henry could be, or anyone else who worked in this building except for the humans. Bay hated how hard it was to understand, but there was nothing he could do about it. That was how things worked for them.

Maybe it was wishful thinking, but Bay couldn't help but hope. And even if Edward wasn't his mate, it didn't mean they couldn't be friends or have a relationship. Bay wasn't going to give up hope, not when he didn't have a reason to.

Chapter Two

The envelopes fell to the floor, skittering around the entrance. Edward stared at the one he was still holding. Seeing Henry's name in big block letters made it hard to breathe. He couldn't believe this. He hadn't expected it. What was he supposed to do with this letter?

Someone had sent an anonymous letter to Henry, and even though Edward had found it, he knew he needed to do something about it. He didn't want to tell his brother, but he had to. If Henry was in trouble, if he was in *danger*, Edward needed him to be aware of it and to do everything necessary to keep himself safe. Edward didn't know what that something would be yet, but it didn't matter.

"Henry?" Edward dropped the keys to his brother's apartment into the glass bowl on the small table in the entrance and abandoned the rest of the envelopes on the floor. There was nothing important in them, anyway. It was just trash, and Henry or Edward would pick it up eventually and throw it away. Edward took his shoes off and left them by the table, then went looking for his brother, who still hadn't answered. That fact made Edward's heart race, and he couldn't help but wonder if Purity had gotten to his brother before he'd arrived. It wouldn't make sense, since he was pretty sure Purity had written the letter he was holding.

"Henry?" he called out again.

"Edward?"

Edward briefly leaned against the wall, relieved that his brother was answering. "Where are you?"

21

Henry's head poked at the kitchen door. "Where do you think I am? What's going on? Why do you sound panicked?" He stepped out of the kitchen, still drying his hands with a towel. "Has something happened? Did someone hurt you?"

Edward couldn't help but smile. This was the big brother he was used to, the protective man who would do everything so that Edward didn't have to worry or be afraid.

But Edward *was* afraid. There was no coming back from the letter he'd found, even though he hadn't opened it.

He hadn't needed to. After the meeting Henry had had with Benedict, they'd had lunch together, and Benedict had explained what had happened to him. That was how Edward knew Benedict had received a similar letter, too, just before he was attacked. Benedict was lucky Dakota was with him, and they all knew it.

Henry didn't have a Dakota, though. He didn't have anyone to protect him, and definitely not Edward, who could never stand up to anyone. He was unable to defend himself or anyone else.

"You're worrying me," Henry said as he walked closer.

Edward swallowed. He held up the letter, and when Henry didn't seem to understand what it was, he explained, "I think this is from Purity."

Henry's eyes widened. "Are you sure?"

"I haven't opened it, so no, but who else would send you this kind of letter?"

"How can you know what kind of letter it is if you haven't seen it?"

Edward gave the letter to his brother, and he saw the exact moment Henry realized he was right.

Just the name and no address meant that whoever had sent this had come to Henry's apartment building. They'd been a few floors away from Henry, and they could have hurt him so easily.

Edward was about to panic, and he knew he couldn't afford to.

Henry handed the envelope back to Edward and rubbed his face. "What now?"

"I don't know." Benedict's first instinct had been to hire a bodyguard. "Maybe you should call Dakota?"

Henry frowned. "What does he have to do with this?"

"He owns a private security company. He knows what's happening, because he and Benedict have been through it already. He'll know what to do."

"I don't want a bodyguard. I don't want someone following me around."

"I realize that, but I don't think you have a choice."

"The letter might not be from Purity."

They both looked at it. Edward was still holding it, and he wanted to drop it. It felt like it was burning his fingers, which of course it wasn't, but that didn't mean he was comfortable holding it, or worse, opening it.

"All right. Maybe we should call Dakota. I don't have his phone number, though," Henry said.

"Call Benedict, then. I know you have his number."

Henry turned around and headed to the kitchen, and Edward followed him. Henry's phone was on the kitchen counter, and he snatched it, unlocking the screen. He apparently had Benedict's number memorized, because he tapped the screen a few times, then put the phone to his ear.

Edward put the letter down on the counter and took a step back. He felt a need to wash his hands, but he stayed where he was, listening to the conversation when Benedict answered. "Benedict? It's me, Henry."

Unfortunately, Edward couldn't hear the other side of the conversation.

"I know. The reason I'm calling you is because of that anonymous letter you told Edward and me about. You remember?"

Once again, there was silence. Henry listened to whatever Benedict was saying, slowly nodding.

Then he said, "Because I just got an anonymous letter, too."

"What?" That one word was loud enough that Edward could hear it even from where he was.

"You heard me. Edward just came in with my mail, and he found an anonymous letter in it. We're not entirely sure it's the same as you got since we haven't opened it, but—"

Edward stared at the envelope on the counter. He wasn't about to touch it, let alone open it. Benedict didn't have to tell him that. Maybe Dakota would be able to use it to get to the people who'd written it. Maybe he could follow the trail up to Purity and get rid of them. Edward didn't even care who was part of Purity. He just wanted them to leave him and his brother alone.

"Of course," Henry said. "We won't touch it again. I'll just put it in a plastic bag and wait."

Benedict was taking control of this. Not that Edward cared. If anything, he felt better. Not only had Benedict received a letter just like this one, but his boyfriend—actually, his mate since he and Dakota had explained to Edward and Henry that they'd found out they were mates—owned a private security company. That meant he was used to this kind of job. He knew what he was doing, and it made Edward feel better.

"He's sending someone," Henry said as he hung up.

Edward nodded at him. "Did he say who?" No matter how terrifying the situation was, Edward couldn't help but wonder if he was about to see Bay again. He didn't even know if he wanted to see the man a second time. They hadn't talked a lot during the meeting between Benedict and Henry, but Edward hadn't been able to ignore Bay. He was pretty sure no one would be able to do that. Bay's personality was too strong, too fascinating.

"He said Dakota himself would come," Henry said. He glared at the envelope. "I really could have done without this."

"So could I. But this is the situation, and we have to deal with it."

"I tried telling Benedict there was no need for him to send Dakota, but he wouldn't listen."

"That's a good thing. I know you don't want to face this because you don't like the consequences, but you *are* in danger. Somehow, Purity found out about what you and Benedict are doing, and they're going to do whatever they can to stop you. They were the ones that attacked Benedict. He was lucky Dakota was with him, but you won't be that lucky if something happens to you. You need a bodyguard, no matter how little you like that."

Henry glared at Edward. "There's no need for you to tell me that." The glare softened, and Henry sighed. "I need to call Lyle. He'll want to know what's happening."

Of course he would want to call Lyle. He was Henry's best friend, although Edward wasn't crazy about him. "You should also call Jessica," he pointed out. "Considering she's your fiancé and everything."

Henry's expression twisted. "Of course. I don't want to scare her, you know?"

Edward nodded, but he couldn't help but wonder why he had to remind his brother to call the woman he was engaged to. He didn't want the answer, though, not right now. Possibly not ever, but if what he suspected was true, he would get details eventually.

He really could have done without a second crisis, but he might get just that.

Bay's phone was ringing, and he stretched off the couch to

grab it from the coffee table. Of course, the coffee table was just a tiny bit too far away, and he didn't always have the greatest balance, so he felt his body tilting forward. He jerked back, but it was too late. He tumbled off the couch, falling face-first onto the carpet.

He huffed and rolled to his back, snatching the phone from the coffee table. He supposed he should feel lucky that he hadn't been far from the floor and the fall hadn't hurt him. "Hello?" he answered without looking at the screen.

"Bay? I need you and Alcott."

Bay sat up at the sound of Dakota's voice. "What happened?" he asked. Because something *had* happened—he was sure of that.

"Edward and Henry Long got an anonymous letter from Purity."

Dammit. Bay had expected something like this might happen, but he wished it hadn't. "Are they okay?"

"Henry sounded shaken, but the, I'm not surprised."

"What do you need me to do?"

"I'm not sure yet, but I'm headed to Henry's apartment to meet them, and I'd like you and Alcott to be with me."

"You think they need a bodyguard."

"One for each of them, yes."

"And you want me and Alcott to be those bodyguards."

"You're my best men."

Bay wasn't sure why it was so important for Dakota and Benedict to keep Edward and Henry safe, but he wasn't about to protest. "I wouldn't mind working with Edward. He and I had a chat while Benedict and Henry talked the other day, and he's a nice guy."

"That's fine with me. You know I don't care who you and Alcott want to stick with, as long as they're not left alone, not after this letter."

"Text me the address, and I'll meet you there." Dakota

would also no doubt call and text Alcott, so Bay didn't have to worry about that.

He was on his feet as soon as the phone call was over. He rushed to his bedroom, changed into jeans and a t-shirt rather than his sweatpants, quickly packed a small bag, and headed out.

He was used to having to rush into missions. It was nothing new, but this time was different. This time, he and Alcott would be protecting people Dakota cared about. Even if he didn't care about them as friends, they were important to Benedict and his business, and Dakota wanted to make sure nothing happened to them.

And of course, there was Edward.

Bay hadn't talked to him since the day of the meeting, but then he hadn't expected to. He also hadn't expected Edward to get a letter from Purity, though. He hadn't expected to become Edward's bodyguard.

Did that mean everything was ruined? He supposed it would depend if Henry officially hired them or if this was a favor Dakota was doing for a friend. Bay knew which one he preferred, but he wasn't about to mention it to Dakota. If Dakota knew he was interested in Edward, he would take him off the case sooner than Bay could say *Edward*, and Bay would be replaced. It might give him a chance to get to know Edward on a personal level, but Bay didn't think so. If this was happening, if the letter was from Purity, Edward and Henry were in trouble.

They wouldn't be allowed to talk to anyone or go anywhere without having gone over the details with their bodyguards first. It would be isolating for them, and Bay hoped it wouldn't last long. Not only did he hate doing that as a bodyguard, but he also hated having to deal with the clients when they weren't happy about it.

Bay was the second to arrive. He wasn't surprised to see

Dakota's car parked in front of the apartment building, and he was lucky enough to find a spot right behind it. He climbed out of his car and locked it, but a voice stopped him before he could head to the door. "How the fuck are you so lucky?" Alcott asked.

He was walking toward Bay, and he was scowling. "What do you mean?"

Alcott gestured at Bay's car. "That. I've been driving around for the past ten minutes, and I wasn't able to find a parking spot, yet you get here, and the car that was parked previously miraculously disappears. How do you explain it?"

Bay grinned at him. "People like me."

"Those people didn't even know you."

Bay enjoyed working with Alcott. He wasn't as close to him as he was to Dakota and Quillan, but that was okay. They worked well together, and he knew they'd be able to keep Edward and Henry safe.

"Did Dakota tell you what this was about?" he asked Alcott as they rode the elevator up.

"He said something about an anonymous letter."

"From Purity, yeah."

Alcott grimaced. "That's not going to be fun."

"Is it ever?" But he was right. Bay hated thinking about Edward being in danger, but that was his reality now. Henry was in danger. Edward might not be, because he wasn't a well-known member of the Long family. People knew he existed, but very few were aware of the role he had in his brother's business. He cared too much for his brother to abandon him, though, and that meant he was right in the thick of it. Bay wouldn't take risks. If Henry had received a letter, it put a target on him and the people close to him, especially Edward.

When Alcott and Bay got to the door of Henry's apartment, it swung open before they could even knock. Dakota stood in front of them, stepping to the side as he gestured them in. "They're in the kitchen. I checked the letter, and it's signed Purity. It's the same as Benedict's, albeit with different wording."

Bay grimaced. He'd expected this, but he wasn't happy about it. "What did Edward and Henry say? How did they react?"

Dakota grimaced. "Not well, especially Henry. Edward seems resigned to his fate, but Henry is still fighting it."

Bay and Alcott exchanged a glance. "He's all yours," Bay said before Alcott could say anything. He wanted to be sure he'd be guarding Edward.

Alcott's glare deepened, but Bay ignored him.

When he and Alcott followed Dakota into the kitchen, Bay knew Alcott would have a fight on his hands.

Henry looked like his head was about to blow up. "I don't want a bodyguard," he said. It seemed to be a conversation he and Dakota were having before Bay and Alcott had arrived.

"You were threatened," Dakota pointed out.

"It's just a letter. It's not going to attack me."

"Maybe not, but this is the way it started with Benedict, and you know what happened after the letter. Do you really want to risk it?"

Henry raked a hand through his hair. "Of course not."

"Benedict would have died if I hadn't been there. He didn't want a bodyguard, either, but his son forced him to accept me, and he did. He was lucky I was by his side when he was attacked. I'm not going to risk either you or Edward."

"Maybe this doesn't have anything to do with what happened to Benedict," Edward said.

Bay was pretty sure he didn't even believe himself, let alone convince the rest of them. "Of course it has to do with what happened with Benedict," he answered.

"Bay is right. The letter's signed by Purity. It's almost identical to the word to the one Benedict received. I need you two to agree to have a bodyguard. Please."

"I don't know if it's worth it," Edward murmured.

"Your *life* is worth it," Dakota said before Bay could yell at Edward not to be stupid. "Your life is worth everything. Trust me. You don't want to take risks in this situation. You can't afford to."

Edward and Henry looked at each other, and Bay held his breath. Even if they said no, he would find a way around it. There was no way he'd allow Edward to be vulnerable, not when Purity was planning to kill him and Henry.

To Bay's relief, Edward slowly nodded as he looked back at Dakota. "Fine. You can assign each of us a bodyguard. We won't protest."

Dakota didn't seem convinced. "You also won't try to ditch them? To convince them to stay away?"

Edward shook his head. "You're right. Our lives are in danger. Even if mine isn't, Henry's certainly is, and I know he's not going to allow a bodyguard to follow him around if I don't. So we're agreeing to this. We need protection, and you know what you're doing. Consider yourself hired."

Edward didn't want someone with him twenty-four-seven, but especially not Bay. He'd only agreed because he knew that Henry would follow his lead. If he said no, Henry would point out that he didn't have a reason to agree to it. But if Edward said yes, then Henry would feel like he had to follow his lead, which was exactly what happened.

Dakota looked relieved. "Right. Okay. Since you both agreed to have a bodyguard, Bay and Alcott will stick by you."

Please, not Bay. Edward knew he wouldn't be lucky,

though. He hadn't missed the way Bay was looking at him, and he suspected that even if Dakota decided to assign Alcott to him, Bay would find a way around it.

He was sure that Bay was good at his job. Dakota wouldn't have called him otherwise. The problem was that for whatever reason, Edward was fascinated by Bay. It wasn't sexual, although Edward couldn't deny that Bay was a beautiful man. He didn't know what it was. He and Bay hadn't spent time together, so they didn't know each other.

Edward wanted that to change, though.

For the first time in forever, he found himself hoping that maybe, just maybe, he could have a relationship. He didn't know if Bay would understand. No one had until now. Edward wasn't even sure he wanted to try. He'd been hurt often enough that the thought terrified him.

But with Bay, he wanted to try. He wanted to become Bay's friend. Of course, now that Bay was his bodyguard, things would probably be different. Bay seemed to be serious when it came to his job, and Edward suspected there might be a *no sleeping with clients or being attracted to them* clause in the contract between Bay and Dakota. That was both a relief and a pity.

"Alcott, you're with Henry," Dakota said.

Edward almost groaned. He'd known this was how things would go. "That means Bay is with me?" he asked.

Dakota nodded. "Don't worry. He's a great bodyguard."

"Oh, I have no doubt." That wasn't Edward's problem. No, his problem was *very* different.

Dakota frowned. "I can call someone else if you want."

"Of course not. Bay and I will be just fine."

"Are you sure? Because you don't look fine."

"I'm still a bit shaken about the letter. But I promise I'm okay."

Dakota still didn't seem convinced, so Edward forced

himself to smile. He couldn't help but hope. He wanted Bay to understand. He wanted Bay to be the one. It didn't make sense, but then, love and relationships rarely did. Otherwise, there wouldn't have been a reason for Edward to fall in love with the assholes he'd been in previous relationships with. But Bay was different. Edward was sure of that. He just didn't know how different, and if it would be enough.

He sucked in a breath. He wanted to think that the letter was just a letter, and he wanted to go home and forget about all of this. He knew better than to try to do that, though. Henry looked like he might be about to throw Alcott and Dakota out, and that would be the worst thing that could happen. Edward needed him to be protected much more than he needed to be protected. Henry was the one in danger here, and Edward would do everything he could to make sure his brother was okay, even accepting a bodyguard he didn't know what to do with.

"How does this work, then?" Henry asked. He was staring at Edward, and Edward could read his expression just as well as if Henry had said words out loud.

If you don't agree to this, I won't either.

Edward rolled his eyes, and Henry shrugged before turning back to Dakota.

"It's not that hard. You two should go on with your everyday lives. Go back and forth between your apartment and your workplace. Alcott and Bay will be with you at all times."

"I suppose we need to go over our schedules with them."

Dakota nodded. "It would be best, yes. They need to know where you're going and how hard it will be to protect you in those places. I'd rather have you stick to either your apartment or your office, but I understand it might not be possible."

Edward snorted softly. "It won't be a problem for me, but it will be for Henry." Henry glared at Edward, but Edward wasn't cowed.

Dakota frowned. "What do you mean?"

"Well, I don't have a social life to speak of. I go from my apartment to the office, then back. The only other places I regularly visit are this apartment and the grocery store. Henry's different, though. He has a best friend he sees often, and of course, he's engaged."

Dakota arched a brow. "Engaged? I didn't find anything about that when I did my research."

Henry laughed. "I should have known."

Dakota shrugged. "You can't say you didn't do your own research on Benedict and me."

"That's why I sent Edward to you. But yes. I am engaged. Her name is Jessica."

"I see. I suppose I should save my breath and not tell you that it would be better for everyone if you stuck to only a few places?"

"I can't exactly abandon her."

"You wouldn't be abandoning her. You would be keeping her safe. You can't know who you'll be with when you're attacked."

"You sound so sure that we *will* be attacked."

Dakota nodded curtly. "That's because I am. You know what happened with Benedict."

"It's different, though."

"Is it? Because it doesn't look like it to me. You're both businessmen. You're both signing deals with people who belong to other elements. That's what Purity doesn't want."

"What *do* they want?" Edward asked. He'd been curious about Purity ever since he'd first heard about them. It was a horrified kind of curiosity, and he wasn't looking forward to the answer.

"Who knows? Even though they're asking that the elements stay away from each other, I suspect there's a lot more to it."

That was what Edward had been thinking. It was a terrifying thought. It would be much easier to dismiss Purity if they knew what was happening, but they didn't. How were they supposed to stop Purity like this? It wasn't their job, but if they didn't do it, who would? Edward wanted to keep Henry safe, and he had no idea where to start.

The conversation got more technical after that. Henry and Edward gave Bay and Alcott all the addresses they thought they would be visiting in the next few days and explained why and what they would be doing there. It was easy in Edward's case. The only places he was planning to visit were his apartment and the office.

He was grateful to be able to leave the apartment. Henry was still talking with Dakota and Alcott, putting things together, but Edward didn't have a role in that conversation. He didn't know how to take his leave without making a scene, though, and he was grateful when Bay noticed how uncomfortable he was feeling and came closer.

"You need to go home?" he asked quietly.

Edward shrugged, then nodded. "I'd like to."

"You're more comfortable when you're at home, aren't you?"

"I am. I'm a quiet person. An introvert. I'd work from home if Henry didn't expect me at the office every day."

"All right. Let's head out, then."

Leaving with Bay was terrifying. Edward had no idea what was about to happen. He didn't know how to behave in Bay's presence. He didn't know what to say or if he should say anything at all. Bay looked focused as he checked the parking garage before nodding at Edward, and Edward didn't want to distract him.

His life was in Bay's hands. He might not be in as much danger as Henry was, but everyone knew that if they wanted Henry to do something, they should use Edward. Edward wouldn't be surprised if someone tried to grab him and use him as leverage, and the thought made him move closer to Bay, who frowned at the move.

"You'll be okay," he said, his voice carrying the promise.

"You can't be sure of that. No offense, because I'm sure you're good at your job, but I can't act like everything is okay when that's not the case."

Bay looked at Edward for a second. "You're right. But I can promise you that I'll do everything in my power to make sure nothing happens to you. And I *am* good at my job. I've been with Dakota since the beginning, and I'm his right hand. He trusts me."

"I trust you, too." Edward didn't know why or even if he should, but God help him, he did.

Bay could see Edward wasn't happy about this, and worse, that he was afraid. He knew there was nothing he could do or say to make it pass, though. He'd hoped his presence with Edward would help, but Edward was still looking around the parking lot as if he expected someone to jump him.

He might not be wrong.

Bay didn't know much about the relationship between the brothers, but he suspected that if anyone wanted to get to Henry, all they'd have to do was hurt Edward. Even though Henry moved around more than Edward did, it would probably be easier to get to Edward anyway. He wasn't in the spotlight like his brother was.

But that was why Bay was here.

They got into the car, Bay in the passenger seat, Edward in the driver's. Edward paused before starting the car and looked at Bay. "How did you get here?"

"My car is parked in front of the building."

"Oh. Should I go there so you can grab it?"

"I'm not leaving you alone."

"What about your car, though?"

"Dakota knows Alcott and I arrived here by car. He'll send someone to bring them to us."

"If you're sure."

"I am." But to Bay, it looked like Edward was trying to avoid spending any length of time with him. "I can call Dakota if you want someone else to be with you."

Edward blinked at Bay. "What do you mean?"

"I don't think you're comfortable having me as your bodyguard. I can ask Dakota to assign someone else to you if you're more comfortable with that."

To Bay's surprise, Edward shook his head. "I'm fine with you. I promise."

"Are you sure?"

Edward tapped his fingertips on the steering wheel. "I'll be honest. It's not you that I'm not comfortable with, but rather with the idea of having a bodyguard. I told you I'm an introvert. In my case, it means that I like being alone. I'm not happy at the thought of having you living in my apartment with me, not because of who you are but because I barely know you. I know there's no other way, though, and honestly, I'd rather have you than a complete stranger."

Bay wasn't offended by Edward's lack of enthusiasm. He wouldn't be happy either if he had to be followed around twenty-four seven and if someone moved into his apartment to keep an eye on him. But Edward was right—there was no other way. Edward was scared. He wasn't used to this kind of situation, and it had to be terrifying. Edward wasn't the target in this case, but it would be too easy for him to become one.

"You don't have to worry about anything," Bay said. "Focus on what you usually do. Go home right now if that's what you would do, or to the office. I'll be the one to adapt to your life, not the other way around."

"But you'll tell me if I do something dangerous?"

"Of course. That's my job. I'll try to accommodate you and your needs as much as I can, but we both know that in some ways, you'll have to change your behavior."

"I'll do it. I need to keep Henry safe, and this is the only way he'll agree to have Alcott with him."

Bay had suspected that was the case. "That's why you agreed to have me with you. Because you wanted Henry to do the same."

Edward sighed and finally turned on the car. "He's stubborn. He's also very protective of me."

"He's your brother. It's normal."

"It's more than that." Edward hesitated. "It's because of our family, or rather, of our father."

"You don't have to talk about this if you don't want to."

"I'm aware of that. I think I need a distraction, though. I've been obsessing over Purity and what they'll do if they manage to get their hands on us, and I can't do that anymore."

Bay nodded. "I'm listening if you want to talk. About anything."

Edward pulled out of the parking lot in silence, but as soon as they were on the road, he said, "Our father loved both of us. He also knew both of us. That's why he left the family business to only Henry."

Bay hadn't been aware of that, although maybe he should have been, since Henry was obviously the one in charge. "Anyone else would have been angry in your place," he pointed out.

"I wasn't, and I never will be. My father made that decision after talking to me. He asked me what I thought about it."

"So you don't want to be in your brother's place."

"I've never wanted it. I already told you I'm an introvert. Can you imagine what it would be like for me to go to meeting after meeting?"

"But you already do. Don't think I don't know that your brother sends you to secret meetings before he steps in."

To Bay's surprise, the corner of Edward's lips curled into a smile. "You're right. He does do that. But we're both okay with it. Honestly, I'm more comfortable working in the shadows. This way, I'm in the family business, but I'm also comfortable."

"So you both got what you wanted."

"We did. But no matter how many times I tell Edward that, he still feels guilty. He feels like our father should have given me a role in the business, and he wants to fix that, even though there's no need for him to."

Bay understood the relationship between the brothers better now. He couldn't say he was surprised. He'd already noticed Henry was the one in charge, the face of the family business. Edward, on the other hand, was more than happy to take a step back.

Bay liked that. As a bodyguard, he needed to stay in the shadows, too. People saw him, but he was never in the spotlight. He also liked it when his clients got used to his presence and either considered him a friend or stopped seeing him outright.

Maybe he and Edward were more similar than he'd thought in the beginning. He supposed he was about to find out. He and Edward were about to spend a lot of time together, no matter how little Edward liked that. Bay had no doubt that Purity would attack the brothers eventually. It was what they'd done with Benedict, and since Henry had no intention of stepping away from the deal, they would try to force his hand. But Alcott would be there, protecting him, and Bay would do the same with Edward.

And if Bay was lucky, he and Edward would get to know each other. He still didn't understand why he was so fixated on Edward, but he didn't think it mattered. Edward seemed to be a good man, and he was gorgeous. It was as good a reason to start a relationship as anything else would be. Not that Bay expected Edward to fall in love with him or anything like that. But if they could be friends, then he wanted that to happen. He wanted Edward to be comfortable with him. It wouldn't be easy, considering that he was now working for Edward, but Bay had never stepped away from difficult decisions or actions.

This situation wasn't any different.

"It's going to take some time to get used to this," Edward murmured.

"But you'll manage. You're strong, Edward. Stronger than you seem to think."

Edward shook his head and gave Bay a sideways glance. "Why are you so sure of me? You have more faith in me than I do."

"I don't know. I don't think it matters, though. Together, we'll keep Purity away." And if they dared come close, Bay would deal with them.

CHAPTER THREE

Edward was walking on eggshells around Bay. He had no idea what to say to the man most of the time, and spending every single day with him was starting to get awkward.

He liked Bay. That wasn't the problem. Bay was a nice man. He was fun, and he gave Edward his space even though he needed to keep an eye on him. He was doing his best so that Edward wouldn't notice him when he was working or doing whatever he needed to do, and Edward was grateful. Still, that didn't change the fact that his apartment felt like it wasn't his anymore. He had to share with Bay, and it was weird. Edward hadn't shared his living space with anyone since he'd left his parents' house, and he hadn't thought he would again.

He'd never moved in with any of his exes. Why should he have? They'd dumped him before things could get that far, and after the first few times, Edward had learned. When he met someone, he always kept a part of him tucked away. He needed to be wary, to make sure that he wouldn't get his heart broken by trusting someone he shouldn't.

So far, he'd never been wrong.

He didn't like to think about the past, but it was hard not to when he was sitting at the breakfast nook pushing his eggs around his plate. He could hear Bay moving around in the guest bedroom, and he was torn between wanting to run away and leave him behind or going to the bedroom and knocking on the door.

He suspected Bay wouldn't mind the second option.

Edward might not be the greatest at relationships, and he was even worse when it came to flirting and realizing that someone was interested in him, but he hadn't missed the long glances Bay gave him. Of course, it might be because of the job, but Edward was pretty sure that watching him didn't involve staring at his ass. He'd caught Bay doing just that a few times, and he was still flustered when he thought about it.

What should he do, though? Technically, Bay was here for a job. He was keeping Edward safe. He wasn't sharing Edward's apartment because he wanted to or because he and Edward were friends. He was here because Edward was in danger. Nothing more.

Or at least, that was what Edward was trying to convince himself of. He was attracted to Bay, even though he didn't want to jump his bones, and he was pretty sure Bay was attracted to him. One of them needed to keep a straight mind, though.

Edward snorted at his own inside joke.

"What's so funny?" Bay asked as he walked into the kitchen.

Edward almost groaned. "You forgot to put on a shirt," he pointed out. He had to look down at his plate so he wouldn't stare, or worse, drool.

There was no denying that Bay's body was gorgeous. Even Edward could admit that. It didn't make his body tingle or anything like that, but he had eyes, and he used them.

Bay looked down at himself. "I'm sorry. Is it bothering you?"

Edward shrugged. "I don't care." That was a lie. He cared, and very much so. He had no idea how to deal with this. He had no idea how to explain to Bay that he was asexual and that it meant they couldn't be together. He didn't even know if he wanted Bay to know. What would happen if Edward told him? Would he at least give Edward the time to explain, or would he run away just like a few of Edward's exes had done? Edward didn't know, and he wasn't feeling up to finding out, not this morning.

"Good." Bay flopped into the seat in front of Edward. "No breakfast for me?" he asked.

Edward pushed his plate toward Bay. "I'm sorry. I wasn't sure you were even in the apartment."

"Of course I was in the apartment." Bay took the plate, and to Edward's surprise, the fork. "I'm not going anywhere without you." He stabbed a piece of egg and stuffed it into his mouth, chewing and humming at the same time.

Edward blinked. "I used that fork."

"So?"

"Nothing." Bay truly was a strange man. "You go ahead and finish the plate. I'm not hungry anymore."

Bay beamed at him as if he'd just offered him a million dollars. "Thank you." He swallowed another forkful of eggs, then asked, "What do you have planned today?"

"The usual. I need to go to the office, and I have a few meetings, all of them in the building." And of course, he had to talk to Henry. Although they hadn't seen each other much in the past few days, Edward hoped it was because they were both trying to get used to having a bodyguard and not for worse reasons.

God knew *he* wasn't used to it yet. Henry might be having an easier time with Alcott, but Edward doubted it. Henry was more outgoing than him, but that didn't mean it wasn't awkward for him, too. He also had to deal with the fact that he was engaged and that Jessica probably spent at least a few nights with him every week, if not more. That couldn't be comfortable.

"Should I plan for your girlfriend coming around?"

Edward was pretty sure he would have dropped his fork if he'd still been holding it. "I'm sorry?"

"Well, I haven't seen anyone around. Your brother is engaged, right?"

"He is, but what does that have to do with me?"

"Probably nothing. But thinking about him made me think about you and about the fact that I haven't met your significant other yet. I thought I would have by now."

Edward had no idea why this was coming out now. "You haven't met my significant other because I don't have one."

Bay chewed, swallowed, then asked, "Why not?"

How was Edward supposed to answer that? He didn't want to lie, but he also didn't want Bay to feel awkward or uncomfortable. "My relationships don't usually last very long," he said. He supposed it was better than blurting out everything.

"Why not? Is it you, or is it them?"

Edward knew that if he said he wasn't comfortable with talking about this, Bay would back off. He always did, which was one of the reasons Edward liked him so much. He didn't want to, though. He and Bay might not be best friends, but he was comfortable with Bay. He hoped Bay could accept him, even though not a lot of people had.

He cleared his throat and wrapped his fingers around his mug of coffee, looking into it rather than at Bay. "I'm asexual." Edward paused, waiting for a reaction. He didn't get the one he expected, though.

After a moment, Bay asked, "So?"

"What do you mean, so?"

Bay put down the fork and cleaned his mouth. "I don't know. I guess I don't understand why you being asexual means your relationships don't last long."

Edward *really* didn't want to talk about this part, but he'd started, so he might as well continue, even though coming out every time he met someone new was exhausting. "How can you not understand? I thought it was obvious." Or at least, it was what everyone thought.

Since Edward was asexual, it meant that he wasn't interested in relationships, right? Edward had heard those words so many times that they were branded in his brain. "You know what being asexual means?" he asked instead of explaining.

Bay tapped his fingertips on the table. "I know it's personal, and that it changes from person to person. And of course, it has nothing to do with sexual orientation."

Edward was surprised, although maybe he shouldn't have been. "You're right. It is different for everyone."

Bay nodded and continued, "Some asexual people are disgusted by sex and don't want anything to do with it. Some don't mind having sex with their partners. Some like some solo action." He looked at Edward. "I'm not about to ask you what *you* like. That's private, and you know where to find me if you want to tell me."

Edward knew he was blushing, but he didn't try to hide it. "Why would I want to tell you?" he asked.

Bay grinned at him. "Why *wouldn't* you? Come on, Edward. I know you can feel it."

Edward shook his head. "It's not possible."

"Why not?"

"It's not." Because Edward couldn't put his heart on the table once again only to have it beaten up. It would hurt especially bad if Bay did something like that because of the kind of man he was. It was also the fact that Bay wasn't going anywhere. Even if Edward didn't want to see him again, he would have to, because Bay was protecting him. He was afraid that if he sent Bay home, Henry would do the same with Alcott, and he couldn't allow that to happen.

Bay leaned over the table and looked Edward in the eyes. "Why don't we talk about it?"

There was nothing Edward wanted less right now, but he

knew there was no escape.

Bay was curious to hear why Edward thought there could be nothing between them. It might be because Bay was his bodyguard, or maybe because Bay wasn't his type. Bay doubted that, though. It wasn't because he was sure of himself, but rather because he'd noticed the way Edward looked at him when he thought he couldn't see it.

"You said you knew what being asexual meant," Edward said.

"I just explained it to you, didn't I?" Then Bay thought about it. "Wait. Are you also aromantic?"

Edward looked nonplussed, but he shook his head. "I'm not. Actually, I think I fall in love too easily."

Bay arched a brow. "Really?" He hadn't thought Edward's cheeks could become any redder, but they did, and he was delighted.

"Really," Edward confirmed. "Usually, it ends badly for me. That's why I don't have a significant other."

Bay could already tell he would want to kill someone by the end of the conversation, but he couldn't resist asking, "Do you want to talk about it?"

Edward shrugged. "Not really, but I suppose you want to anyway."

"I do. It doesn't mean you have to, though."

"Maybe I think you'll understand. Maybe that's why I'll tell you even though I'd rather go to the dentist."

"I already do understand, but I'm curious. Again, though, we don't have to have this conversation. It might help you, but I won't push." And if there was one thing Bay was eager to do, it was helping Edward.

Edward sucked in a breath. "You know, in the beginning, when I tell people I'm asexual, they're intrigued. A lot of them ask questions, usually questions you wouldn't ask anyone else, like what I enjoy doing in bed, things like that. I liked that you didn't assume that I didn't enjoy anything."

Bay was doing his best not to open his big mouth and ask Edward *exactly* what he liked between the sheets. He was curious. Of course he was. He was attracted to Edward, and the fact that Edward wasn't attracted to him the way he was and that he didn't want to fuck him didn't bother him.

He might be a guy, but that didn't mean his dick ruled him.

"I don't like to assume anything," he said.

Edward nodded. "Well, thank you. But while I'm not disgusted by sex, I don't care about it, either. And that's been a problem in my relationships. I think in the beginning, a lot of people want to see if they can change my mind. Some guys seem to think that I'm asexual only because I've had bad experiences with sex. They think I don't know what I like, and they couldn't be more wrong."

Bay was kind of horrified, but he wasn't surprised that some dickheads thought they could change Edward. They didn't understand that being asexual was part of Edward and that it was nothing he could or should change. Edward was perfect the way he was.

"So that's why your relationships don't usually end well," Bay said.

"It is. I tend to get crushes and fall in love too easily. I guess I'm romantic. I *want* to be in love. But everything always comes crashing down when the person I'm with realizes that no matter how much they push, I won't fall into bed with them." Edward looked Bay in the eyes. "And that won't change. Whoever I end up spending the rest of my life with, if there even is such a person out there, will have to get used to the idea that sex is just not for me. I've tried it, several times, and I'm done with it. I don't care how bad or good my past experiences where. It doesn't change how I feel or the fact that

I don't experience sexual desire."

Bay wanted to get his hands on the people who'd hurt Edward. His job was to protect Edward after all, even though it wasn't from dickheads. "I understand." That was all he could say or do.

"Do you?"

"You know how Dakota likes to hire different elements?"

Edward frowned. "We've already talked about that, yes."

"Well, he likes to have a diverse workforce. And I'm not talking only about elements. He doesn't care about people's sexualities, and he doesn't let that stop him from hiring people. I might be gay, but I work with people who are bisexual, pansexual, you name it, we probably have it. That's why I don't care about what you're telling me. Being asexual doesn't change anything about you. It doesn't make you any less gorgeous."

Edward looked away. "It does change things, though. When people realize I won't suddenly want to have sex with them, they usually leave."

"They're assholes." Edward barked out a laugh, and Bay smiled at him. "You know I'm right," he added.

"It doesn't make it easier to accept, though."

"Maybe not. But you're going to have to trust someone eventually. You know there's someone for you out there."

"My mate."

"Your mate, but not just that. With how hard it is for us to find our mates, we might never stumble onto them. I don't know about you, but even though I hate the thought of not finding my mate, I'm not going to wait around for him forever. I want to live my life, and if I never meet him, I don't want to have regrets by the time I'm eighty. I want to fall in love. I want a relationship. I want to build a life with someone I love." Edward deserved so much better than what he'd been given until now. Bay wanted to be the one to give that to him, but he could see that Edward was uncomfortable.

It made sense. He'd trusted people with who he was and with his heart, and they'd betrayed him because he wasn't exactly the kind of person they wanted to be with. Of course he didn't want to try again. It didn't matter that Edward was young. He might have all the time in the world to find someone to spend the rest of his life with, since he was only thirty-four, but it was obvious he was lonely.

Bay had been with him for a few days, and so far, they'd only been at the apartment and at the office. The only people Edward had spoken to were his brother and a few people at the office. The only meaningful conversations he'd had were with Henry.

No matter how introverted Edward was, it had to be a lonely life. Of course, Bay might be wrong. He was used to being around people. He didn't know what loneliness was like. Maybe Edward wasn't lonely so much as he liked being alone.

But even if that were the case, he deserved to be loved. He had a good heart, and he was the sweetest man Bay had ever known. He should be happy, and even though that happiness didn't have to come through a man or a relationship, it didn't mean having love in his life wouldn't help.

Bay opened his mouth to tell Edward that and so much more, but the sound of a key turning in the lock of the front door made him snap his mouth shut. He looked at Edward, frowning. "Were you expecting anyone?"

Edward shook his head. "We just talked about the fact that I don't *have* anyone to expect. It's probably Henry, though. He's the only one who has a key."

"No one else has one?"

"Well, my mother, but she's on a cruise right now. It can't be her."

Bay nodded and started to rise from the chair, but Edward

put a hand on his arm and shook his head. "Really. It's Henry. It can't be anyone else."

"You can't be sure of that."

"Check your phone. Alcott would have texted you if Henry was headed this way, wouldn't he?"

Edward was right. Bay slid the phone out of his pocket and peered at it. He hadn't even felt it vibrate while he was talking with Edward, but Edward was right. He had several messages from Alcott, all of them giving him an update of how close he and Henry were to the apartment.

Bay relaxed. "You're right. It's Henry and Alcott."

Edward relaxed. "Told you so."

Bay wished they could continue their conversation, but it wasn't the case with Henry here. Whatever the reason was for his presence, the brothers would probably need some time on their own, and that was more than okay with Bay.

He pushed away from the table and rose to his feet. "I think I'm going to go to the guest bedroom and grab a shirt. You might not have a problem with me being shirtless, but your brother will probably see things differently."

Henry stumbled into the kitchen just then, and Bay frowned. Something was wrong. He didn't know what, although he was sure it didn't have anything to do with Purity. Alcott would have warned him otherwise. Knowing that wouldn't help Bay much, though.

Edward was relieved when Henry walked into the kitchen, but the relief only lasted a few seconds. He could tell something was wrong with his brother at first sight, and he jumped from his seat, rushing toward Henry. Henry wouldn't want to do this where Bay and Alcott, who'd come in after him, could hear. That was why Edward grabbed his brother's wrist and dragged him toward his bedroom.

It was the only room into which Bay never followed him. He regularly checked it, but it was still Edward's sanctuary, and Edward felt better as soon as the door was closed behind them.

Henry still hadn't said anything. Edward looked at him, trying to understand what was wrong. He was pale, and there were dark shadows under his eyes as if he hadn't slept enough last night, or maybe not at all.

Edward swallowed. "Is it Purity?" he asked.

Henry shook his head. The movement was almost enough to topple him off his feet. Edward knew he couldn't be weak, not physically, not when he'd been fine yesterday, but whatever had happened had hurt him, so much so that he looked like he might faint.

Edward stepped closer and gently pushed his brother until he could sit on the bed, then he crouched in front of him and looked up at him. "Talk to me. I can't help you if you don't."

Finally, Henry's expression shifted. He rubbed his face with both hands, then looked bleakly at Edward. "Jessica and I decided to see if we were mates last night," he confessed.

Edward sucked in a breath. "Why?" he asked.

Henry shrugged. "She wanted to know. She insisted."

Edward shook his head. He wasn't going to berate his brother for what had happened, but he could tell that Edward had known this would be a bad idea. "You knew what the odds were, Henry," he murmured.

"I did. But she'd been asking for months, and I couldn't say no anymore."

"She insisted?" Henry wasn't surprised. He knew Jessica, and he liked her. He was aware of the fact that she viewed soulmates as a romantic thing, and while it was, it could also be hard when two people realized they *weren't* mates.

Which was clearly precisely what had happened.

Edward sighed. "What now?" He wanted to say he was

sorry, but Henry already knew that, and Edward doubted he would be happy to hear the words.

"I don't know. She left the apartment last night. She was crying."

Edward wasn't surprised at that, either. "She'll be okay. I mean, I know it was a huge blow for her, but a lot of people are with someone even though they're not their mates. It doesn't mean anything. It doesn't mean you don't love her or that she doesn't love you. Give her some time. Things will get better."

Henry looked at Edward. "Really? Because it doesn't feel like it right now."

What was Edward supposed to say to that? He wanted to reassure his brother, but he wasn't sure he could. He didn't like that Jessica had left instead of talking things out. She was hurt, but so was Henry, and neither of them had done any-thing wrong. "Don't make any kind of decisions right now. You need to wait and listen to what she has to say when she contacts you."

Henry laughed darkly. "She texted me this morning."

From his tone, it wasn't a good thing. "What did she say?"

"That she needs time. That this wasn't what she expected. That our relationship isn't what it was before we found out."

Edward settled on the floor with his legs crossed as he tried to find something to say. "Dammit. Did she break up with you?"

"It sure sounds like it, doesn't it?"

"I don't know. She never said that things were over, did she?"

"She didn't, but I know how important this was to her. It's over, Edward. I'm sure of it."

It was the last thing they needed. They already had enough problems with Purity coming after them. Edward was still waiting for the other shoe to drop, and he knew that it *would* drop. It was only a matter of time and of where and when. And now Henry was distracted. He probably wouldn't notice if someone came for him, not in the state he was in.

Edward supposed he should be relieved that Henry had Alcott. But no matter how good Alcott was at his job, he was still just a man. He couldn't work miracles or be everywhere at once.

Edward rubbed the back of his neck, trying to come up with something to say that would make Henry feel better. He wasn't sure there was anything, though. "Why don't you ask her what's next?"

Henry shook his head. "She wants to be left alone."

"Of course she does, and I get why. But she's not the only one in this relationship, and what you need right now is an answer. I'm not saying that you should push for it. I understand why she needs time. But if she's planning on breaking up with you, she needs to tell you at least. She can't leave you in limbo the way she is right now."

Henry's eyes narrowed. "You want me to call her after she told me to leave her alone?"

"That's not what I said. Text her. Ask her what's going on. Tell her how sorry you are that the two of you aren't mates and that it doesn't change anything for you."

"I don't know that it doesn't," Henry said.

This was what Edward had been afraid of. "You wanted her to be your mate."

Henry rolled his eyes. "We were engaged. I wanted her to be my mate. I hoped she was."

"You didn't want to check, though. You said she was the one who insisted."

"I didn't want to find out if we weren't. I was afraid that was the case. I love her, and I know she loves me, but what were the odds? People don't find their mates easily. Why should it have been any different for us?"

He was right. Edward knew that if he ever was lucky enough to find someone to share his life with, he would never want to find out if they were mates. He didn't think he could take the crushing disappointment if they weren't, and what had just happened with Henry and Jessica was exactly what he wanted to avoid.

He didn't know what this meant for them, but he could imagine all too well. Just like Henry had said, they would probably break up.

It was a pity. Henry had been happy with her, and they'd been looking forward to the wedding. Hell, everything was already booked, and Edward couldn't help but resent the fact that mates were a thing. Who cared if someone was perfect for you? Who decided that, anyway? Was it a biological thing, or was there someone in the sky looking down at them and using them as pawns?

Edward didn't care, and he wished Henry and Jessica didn't, either. Henry wouldn't be hurting as much as he was right now if they didn't.

"You have to talk to her," he repeated. "Even if it's to check whether she wants to break up with you. But if you love her, and I know you do, you'll need to try to convince her that you don't care whether or not you're mates. I know you said you're not sure about that, so before calling her, think about it. Does knowing that she's not your mate change things between you?"

"I don't know. I want to say no. It doesn't change how much I love her, or the woman she is. But can I marry her knowing that there's someone else out there for me?"

Edward reached out and gently slapped his brother's thigh. "I sure hope you can, because you don't know if you're ever going to meet your mate, and if you do, you won't even know that you have unless you try to mix your powers. Do you want to ruin one of the best things in your life because of that? For a dream you might not achieve?"

Henry was to the point of tears when he looked at Edward. "I don't know, Eddie. I don't know anything right now."

Edward's heart broke a little. If he could, he would take all the pain away from his brother. But he couldn't, so instead, he leaned against Henry's legs and hoped that eventually, everything would be okay.

"What happened?" Bay asked as he rose from his chair.

Alcott shrugged. "Not sure. It has to do with his girlfriend, though."

"You mean his fiancée. They're engaged."

"Whatever. She left crying last night, and I hadn't seen Henry until he came out of his bedroom and told me he was coming here."

Bay leaned against the table, trying to think about what could have caused this. "Did they fight?"

"Not as far as I know. I didn't hear anything, but then, I try very hard not to when she comes over."

"Walk me through what happened."

Alcott rolled his eyes, but he obeyed. "She arrived last night, and I opened the door for her. She has a key, but you know I like to control who comes in and out of the apartment. She looked excited, almost bouncing on her feet. I didn't ask her what was happening because it's not my business. Henry came out to greet her, and they disappeared into his bedroom. I have no idea what happened while they were inside, and I don't want to know. I didn't hear screaming or anything that would have made me intervene. I went to the living room to watch TV, and the next thing I know, I hear a door slam, and she rushed out of the bedroom, crying. Henry went after her, but she ignored him and left."

"Did you ask him what happened?"

"Of course. I also checked his bedroom to make sure no one was there. He wasn't happy about that and told me to fuck off."

It wasn't the first time someone told Alcott that, and it wouldn't be the last. "He said nothing about what happened with his fiancée?"

"No," Alcott confirmed. "He just went back to his bedroom and stayed there until this morning. You have any questions?"

Bay shook his head. He had about a dozen questions, but he realized it wasn't his business. Whatever had happened between Henry and his fiancée, it had nothing to do with him. As long as it didn't put Edward in danger, he wasn't going to pry.

He thought he and Edward had taken a step forward during breakfast, and he wished Henry hadn't barged in. He wanted to see where things were going, but since they'd been interrupted, he wasn't sure he could get them back on track, or if he should hope he could.

He was grateful that Edward had felt comfortable enough with him to tell him that he was asexual. He was also angry that Edward's exes had been dickheads, but that didn't matter anymore. Now, Edward had Bay, even though he didn't want to acknowledge it yet. Bay was conflicted, too. This was supposed to be nothing more than a job for him, but he'd known it wouldn't be the case right from the beginning. He should have told Dakota, but he hadn't.

And now he was falling in love with Edward.

Bay and Alcott settled into the living room to watch TV with the volume turned down so they could hear if something happened in the bedroom. Nothing did, though, and after a while, Edward and Henry came out. They had to go to the office, and they were already late. It was going on nine AM, and Bay knew it had to be torture for Edward, even though the reason he was late was that his brother and boss had needed him. He was one of those annoying people who were always punctual, who usually arrived early, while Bay was the opposite. He'd learned to be on time, but it didn't work every time, and it was always a bother.

He rose from the couch and looked at Edward, trying to understand if something had happened. "Everything okay?" he eventually asked because he needed to be sure.

Edward nodded, then shook his head, then nodded again. That wasn't useful at all.

"We're okay," Henry snapped. "And we're ready to go to the office."

"We can go whenever you're ready," Bay said. He didn't want to spend any length of time with Henry right now, though. The man looked like he was walking a thin line between being pissed at the world and sad. Bay didn't want to be in the crosshairs when he exploded, and he didn't doubt that would happen eventually.

Bay bit his lower lip. He knew he shouldn't be doing this, but he couldn't help it. "Do we *have* to go to the office today?" he asked.

Both Henry and Edward blinked at him, and at that moment, he saw the resemblance between the brothers. Henry was taller and broader, and there was an air of authority to him, while Edward was smaller and appeared gentler. Bay knew which brother he preferred, and which brother he hoped would be part of his life for a long time.

"What do you mean?" Edward asked cautiously.

Bay gestured at Henry. "It's obvious something happened, and before you become angry at me, I don't want to know what it was. It's your business, and as long as it doesn't have to do with Purity, Alcott and I don't need to know. But like I said, something happened, and I don't think you'll be able to focus on your work today. Can you take a day off? Both of you. You've been working hard." Edward even worked on Sundays, which Bay was used to, but didn't like. Edward deserved to rest, but he never did. He worked every single day of the week, late into the night.

"We can't afford to take the day off," Edward said.

"I think we can," Henry interrupted. Edward looked at him like he'd grown a second head, but Henry ignored him. "It's not a bad idea. I'll be distracted. You know I will. I don't want to cause a disaster because I was thinking about last night and do something I shouldn't have. One day won't kill us, and it won't destroy the company."

"Are you sure? Because we have those contracts to go over, and I have a meeting—"

"Call your secretary and ask her to move the meeting back. I'm sure that whoever you have the meeting with won't mind seeing you tomorrow, or the day after that."

Edward still didn't look convinced, but Henry was on board. He was a bit more excited than he'd been earlier, and Bay counted that as a win.

"If you're sure," Edward finally said.

Henry nodded. "You're right. I need time to figure things out, and so does Jessica. I know that if I go to the office, I'd need to focus entirely on work and not think about this, and that's not going to happen. I need to find balance and an answer. Maybe taking a day off will help with that."

As Henry and Alcott headed outside the apartment with no goal in mind, Edward moved closer to Bay. "Thank you," he murmured.

"What are you thanking me for?" Bay asked even though he knew.

Edward looked at his brother, who seemed to have more of a spring in his step than before. "He needed this. If I had suggested it, he would have said no. But for whatever reason, he seems to listen to you and Alcott more than he does to me, and what you said helped."

"I could tell something bad happened."

"You're right. It's something that could change Edward's entire future, and he doesn't know how to deal with it."

"Are you sure it has nothing to do with Purity?"

"It doesn't. It's private."

Bay hesitated. He knew that whatever was happening to Henry wasn't his business, but since he was angling for a relationship with Edward, he wanted Edward to know that he was there for him. "I know you probably won't, but you can talk to me if you need to. I won't tell anyone."

Edward looked at him. "Thank you. I don't know if I will, not right now anyway. But maybe tomorrow? I need to focus on Henry today."

It made sense. "Of course. It's an offer that won't change. You know where to find me if you want to talk."

Edward laughed, and Bay couldn't help the grin that bloomed on his face in answer. "You're right. I know exactly where to find you if I need you," Edward agreed.

Even if Bay didn't manage to do anything else today, at least he'd made Edward laugh. That was all Bay wanted from life right now—for Edward to be happy and safe.

He was still working on the second one.

CHAPTER FOUR

Edward was worried about Henry. There was nothing new to that, even though Edward was the younger brother, but he'd been especially worried since Henry and Jessica had fought two weeks earlier. Henry had been down, which wasn't surprising, but Edward wished he could do more to distract his brother. Of course, the fact that Purity hadn't written them another letter was also worrying. Some people would think it was because they'd forgotten about them, but Edward doubted that was the case. Purity didn't feel like the kind of association who forgot about people. He knew they were watching, and the thought gave him the creeps. He also hated having to wait until they acted again. So far, it had only been a letter. The next time, it would be much worse.

"What's going on in that head of yours?" Bay asked.

Edward shook himself. He needed to be more careful. He needed to pay attention, even though Bay was there. He knew Bay could protect him, but that didn't mean he would be able to save him if something happened. He might be hurt, or worse, and then, Edward would be on his own, and he would have to deal with that.

But he didn't want to think about Bay not being there anymore. He didn't think he could deal with that, too — not now, and not ever.

"Edward? Can you hear me?" Bay sounded even more worried than he had a few seconds ago, and Edward didn't want him to be.

He forced himself to smile. "I'm fine. Just thinking about

Henry."

Bay grimaced. "How's he doing? I haven't asked, because I know how hard it must be for him to go through this, but I want both him and you to know that I'm here if you need to talk to me."

Edward's heart fluttered in his chest. It wasn't surprising that Bay was worried about Henry. It was just the kind of man he was. Even though Henry wasn't his assignment, Bay still wanted him to be okay. "I'm not sure. He's not talking to me."

"That's not a surprise. Alcott told me he and Henry are leaving the office now, too."

It was a surprise. Henry had started working long hours since he and Jessica had broken up. To be honest, Edward didn't know if the engagement was off or not, and he wasn't sure they knew, either. What he did know was that they weren't talking to each other, and that couldn't be good. Edward might not be an expert at relationships, but even he knew that if a couple needed to patch things up, they had to talk to make it happen. He didn't know if Henry or Jessica was avoiding it, but he didn't think it mattered. The result was what it was, and they wouldn't be able to solve their problems if they didn't see each other.

But maybe it was easier for them to ignore everything. He would probably feel the same way if he were in their place, and he was grateful he wasn't.

"That's good," he murmured. He couldn't help but wonder what Henry would do at home, though. He knew that the reason Henry had started working so late was because he didn't know what to do with himself once he got home. Alcott was there, of course, but he wasn't a friend. No matter how friendly he was, he was still a bodyguard.

Edward didn't think that Henry and Alcott's relationship was like the one between him and Bay. Not that he and Bay had a relationship beyond Bay protecting him, not yet anyway. But even though they hadn't spoken about what was growing between them again since the day Edward had told Bay he was asexual, Edward couldn't ignore it anymore. Something was growing between them, and even though so far, they'd both avoided talking about it—for wildly different reasons, no doubt—eventually, they would have to. That meant that Edward needed to make a decision. The problem was that he couldn't seem to be able to think. Between work, Purity, and Henry, his mind was always occupied by something. He needed to take some time to think about himself, but it felt impossibly hard right now.

But Bay wasn't pushing, and Edward was grateful. He knew Bay wouldn't demand anything from him. He was focused on his job and Edward's safety first, and everything else would come later. It was both a relief and incredibly frustrating, because Edward wanted more.

He just had to deal with his own feelings first.

When he and Bay got to the cars, Alcott and Henry were already there. To Edward's surprise, they were leaning toward each other, quietly speaking. Henry jerked when he heard Edward and Bay, and he took a step back. Edward blinked at his reaction, making a mental note that he would have to ask his brother what was going on.

He had no doubt Henry would try to avoid answering, but Edward had experience with this. He wanted an answer, and he would get one.

"Everything okay?" Bay asked as they reached the other two.

Alcott nodded. "I checked the car. Nothing to report."

"Good." He turned toward Edward. "Get in."

Edward frowned. "Are Henry and Alcott coming with us?" That would explain why they were standing next to a limousine. Edward hated riding in that kind of car, but it was the only one that was big enough for them. There was even a driver who was waiting by the driver's door, looking at them nervously.

"Yes. We think it's safer."

Something had happened. That was the only reason for them to ride together. They had never done that until now, but Edward knew from Bay's expression that even if he asked, he wouldn't get an answer.

So he obeyed. Part of him wanted to push back, but he wasn't stupid. He knew that whatever was happening, Bay and Alcott were doing this to keep him and Henry safe, which was the only thing that mattered.

Edward slipped into the backseat and waited until Henry was beside him to turn to him. "Talk to me," he said.

Henry grimaced. "I don't want to."

"I know. But you have to. I won't say you'll feel better, because I don't think that's the case, but at least it'll be out there, and I might be able to help you. I can't until I know what's going on."

Henry rubbed his face. He peered at the seats in front of them, but thankfully, Alcott and Bay were talking. They were on high alert, looking this way and that and not paying attention to what Edward and Henry were doing.

Something had *definitely* happened.

Edward turned his attention back to Henry and waited. He knew that asking again wouldn't change anything. If Henry was going to talk to him, he would do it because he wanted to, not because Edward pushed too hard.

Henry sighed and looked at Edward. "Jessica called me."

That would explain why Henry looked like he hadn't slept in several days. "What did she say?"

From Henry's expression and the way he looked, Edward doubted it was good. Still, no matter how bad Henry was hurting, at least he knew what was happening. It was better than waiting for Jessica to take the next step.

Henry shook his head. "Please. Can we not do this now?"

"We can wait until we're home, if you want." Although Edward wasn't sure which home they were going to. "But I do want you to talk to me, please. I know it's hard. I wouldn't be pushing if I didn't think it was important."

The corner of Henry's lips curled into a half-smile. "But you already know I won't feel better after I'm done telling you what's happening."

"That's because I know it'll take you a while to feel better. But I want to be there for you. If you don't want to talk, then don't. I do hope that you have enough trust in me to let me know, though."

Henry chuckled. "You're playing dirty. You already know I trust you." He sucked in a breath and opened his mouth.

The car abruptly stopped.

Edward and Henry looked at each other. "What's going on?" Edward asked, turning toward Bay. "We can't be home already. It hasn't been long enough."

Bay nodded curtly. "You're right. I don't think we're home."

Edward bit his lower lip. "Does that mean we're in trouble?"

Bay's expression was grim. "It's probable, yes."

Bay had no idea what was happening, but he was pissed. Like Edward had said, they couldn't be home already, and they weren't supposed to make a stop before arriving at the apartment building. They were going home because Purity had sent Henry another letter, even more menacing this time, and Dakota had agreed that it would be better if Edward and Henry hid away for a few days.

He turned in his seat and tried to look at the driver, but the glass between the back area and the driver seat was raised, and he couldn't see anything.

He looked at Alcott. "What do you think?" he asked.

Alcott shook his head. "Nothing good."

Bay shared that opinion. He tried to think about what to do, but it was hard when Edward was in the car with him. Edward was in danger, and Bay couldn't seem to be able to focus on anything else. This was why he shouldn't have allowed himself to fall in love with Edward.

That was easier said than done, though.

Bay needed to focus. If he didn't, Edward might get hurt, or worse, and he wouldn't be able to live with himself.

"Okay," he said. "We can't stay here."

"Agreed," Alcott said. His voice had gone hard, and Bay was grateful to have him with him on this occasion. He would probably have been able to deal with the situation if he'd been alone, but it was always better to have someone at his back.

"Who's going out?"

"Both of us." Alcott looked at Henry and Edward, who were huddled on the seat in front of them. "You two need to stay in here until we tell you to leave. Understood?"

Edward and Henry both nodded. They slid closer to each other, and even though they weren't hugging yet, it was a close thing.

Bay and Edward exchanged one more glance, then Bay reached for his door and opened it.

They weren't where they were supposed to be. They were supposed to be heading to Henry's apartment building, but instead, they were in what looked like an abandoned warehouse. Bay couldn't tell what had been happening in here before it had been abandoned, though. The warehouse was entirely empty, and his footsteps echoed in the wide space.

The driver was still huddled in his seat, but before Bay could ask him what the fuck was happening, people seemed to pop out from everywhere at once.

Bay and Alcott were overwhelmed quickly. There was no other way to say it. They were trained, though, so it didn't stop them.

Bay punched a man and kicked a second one. He took a punch to the stomach that folded him in two for a second, but he knew that he needed to focus and pushed through. It was the only way he would be able to save Edward.

Edward. Bay jumped when he heard the scream. He knew it was Edward before he turned around to look, and when he did, he wasn't surprised to see that two men had managed to drag Edward and Henry out of the car. They were both putting up a good fight, though. Edward was fighting like a wildcat, trying to punch and kick to the best of his ability. He was one against two, though, and there wasn't much he could do. Still, he was trying, and Bay's chest expanded with pride.

"Edward and Henry," he yelled at Alcott.

Alcott's head snapped toward the car, and his expression hardened. Before Bay could say anything else, Alcott rushed toward the limo, and Bay could only follow him.

He was thankful he had when they reached the car. A man was about to punch Edward in the face, and Bay got there just in time to grab the man's wrist and pull him back. Edward's eyes were wide with panic and fear, but he nodded at Bay, and to Bay's surprise, he placed himself behind him, back to back so they could both face their attackers.

Air, water, and earth erupted. Their little group didn't have control over fire, but Bay was confident they didn't need it to win. They only had to clear a path through the people attacking them and get out of the warehouse. Once that was done, they would be safe—ish. He doubted they'd be entirely safe until they reached either Edward or Henry's apartment, but it would be better than being stuck in this warehouse with a bunch of people trying to hurt them.

Fights were always confusing, but especially so with

elements flying around.

"There are no roots!" Edward yelled.

Bay realized he'd reached down with his power, trying to find roots under the thick cement under their feet. He wasn't surprised he couldn't find anything. "Focus on the earth! Use it to shield the rest of us so we're not hit. We'll take care of Purity while you protect us." Bay had no doubt that their attackers were part of Purity. The attack was too similar to the one Dakota and Benedict had gone through to be anything else.

The cement cracked and broke as Edward raised earth shields around them. Bay knew he couldn't keep them up for long. He didn't have to, though. While he made sure the rest of them weren't being hit, they were working on kicking their attacker's asses.

Alcott was throwing people around, using his power over the air to make sure they didn't get back up, slamming them against walls and the ground. Henry had noticed what Edward was doing and had added his own power to it, keeping Alcott and Bay even safer as they focused on the enemy.

Bay grinned and went to work.

His power was over water, and while there wasn't a large amount of it around, he'd trained for years to be able to use the little that was in the air. It took a lot of focus, but having to protect Edward was enough for Bay to be able to do that. He needed the four of them to get out of here alive, and unhurt if at all possible.

He gathered all the water he could find, created a bubble of it over their head, then threw it at the men rushing them. While they were spluttering and distracted, he reached out for the water in their bodies.

Bay hated doing this. He didn't like killing people, but this was a particularly horrific way to go. Still, he sucked all the water out of the men's bodies, and he watched as they mummified—alive. Their screams would add to the ones that already woke Bay up at night, but it was okay. He would deal with it when he had to.

"Watch out!" Alcott yelled.

Bay turned around. It only took him a second to understand what was happening, and when he did, he grabbed Edward, twisted them so Edward would be under him, and dropped to the ground.

The limo exploded.

Someone had thrown a ball of fire toward it—toward *them*—and hadn't thought of the consequences. Bay's back hurt like hell, and he knew he was burned, but it didn't matter. He peered down, making sure Edward was safe. He was the important one, and Bay *needed* him to be okay.

Bay couldn't hear anything except the roar of the explosion. He curled himself into a tighter ball around Edward. He knew that some parts of Edward's body were exposed, but there was only so much he could do. He was doing his best. He'd already failed Edward today when he hadn't realized that the driver wasn't taking them home. He wouldn't fail him again.

It hurt. His back was exposed to the explosion, and even though they'd been far enough away that they weren't killed, debris and heat still pelted him. He couldn't even focus long and hard enough to use water, not when the only thing his brain could say was *keep Edward safe, keep Edward safe*.

Bay was in love with him. He couldn't deny it anymore, and he promised himself that if they both made it out of this alive, he would tell Edward. Whatever Edward's answer would be, he needed to know. Bay needed him to be aware of it.

But of course, they would have to make it out alive first, and Bay wasn't sure that would be the case.

Everything hurt. Edward wasn't even sure he was still in one piece, and he didn't know if he wanted to find out, either. He was broken, or God forbid, if *Bay* was broken, he wouldn't be able to take it. He didn't know what he would do, but he'd wouldn't be pretty. That was why he needed both of them to be okay, and of course, Henry and Alcott, too.

His ears still roared with the sound of the explosion when Bay rolled off him. He heard Bay yelp, and he scrambled to his feet, ready to protect him if he needed to. He might not be a bodyguard like Bay, but this, he could do.

"Bay?" he asked. He could barely hear his own voice. He knelt next to Bay, who was sitting up and grimacing.

"I'm fine."

Edward snorted. "You don't look fine."

"Okay, so maybe I'm hurt. But I'll be okay. I promise."

Edward knew they couldn't promise that. How could he? But for now, it was enough, or rather, it would have to be. "Are you sure? I can try to find someone."

Bay shook his head. "There's no one here, Edward. It's why they brought us here."

He was right. There was no one else in the warehouse, not anymore. The only people still there were dead, and Edward carefully avoided looking at their bodies. He looked around, trying to find Henry and Alcott, then cried out when he finally saw them. They were in pretty much the same position he and Bay had been, with Alcott curled around Henry, pinning him to the ground. They weren't moving, and Edward scrambled to his feet. He needed to get to them. He needed to get to Henry.

"Wait," Bay said.

When Edward turned to him, intent on telling him that he had to get to his brother, he saw that Bay was trying to get up. He was hurt, though, and obviously in pain. It made

Edward's chest squeeze, and he reached out, helping him to his feet. "You should stay down," he said anyway.

"I can't. We need to check on Alcott and Henry."

So together, they went. Bay was walking easily enough, but it was obvious that every step he took was painful. There was nothing Edward could do to help, though, so he focused on getting to Henry.

He didn't know what he would do if Henry was hurt, or worse, dead. He didn't know if he could deal with it. He was relieved that Bay was okay, but this wasn't over yet, and he didn't know if it ever would be.

He almost fell to his knees when he got to Alcott and Henry and heard Henry groaning. He was pretty sure it was Henry, anyway, and he knelt next to them, ready to roll Alcott off if he needed to.

Alcott was in pretty much the same shape as Bay. Part of his jacket had been burned, and Edward's stomach turned at the sight of pink and red skin under it. It would hurt, but he should be okay.

"Alcott?" Bay asked as he crouched next to them.

Alcott rolled to his back, then he winced and jerked into a sitting position. "Fuck. That hurts." He looked around. "Where are they?"

"Either dead or ran away. How are you? How's Henry?"

Edward reached for his brother. Henry was sitting up, too, and while he was covered with dirt, he seemed to be okay. "What happened?" he asked.

"A dumb fire wielder decided to make the car explode," Alcott snapped. His expression softened. "I'm sorry."

Henry shook his head. "Don't be. I'm pretty sure you saved my life just now."

Edward had to sit down. He plopped on his ass, not even caring that the floor was hard and covered in debris that dug into his flesh. His knees didn't feel like they could hold him up anymore, and he didn't want to risk it. He'd probably hit his head if he fainted or something, and he would be in an even worse position than he was now.

"I'm calling Dakota," Alcott said as he reached for his jeans pocket.

Edward didn't miss the wince on his face, but he focused on Henry. "How are you? Really?"

"I've been better."

Edward snorted. "I bet. So have I. Anything broken?"

Henry shook his head. "I don't think so." His eyes were wide when he looked at Edward. "I thought I was going to die. How are *you*?"

"In one piece, which is the best I could hope for, considering what just happened."

"You're not wrong about that."

Edward got to his feet, then helped Henry to his. They hugged carefully, knowing that they could make things worse. By the time they were done, Dakota's team had already arrived. It was impressive, but Edward couldn't think of anything but going to bed. Well, he wanted to shower first, but he needed rest and not to have to think about the people who'd died today.

He was conflicted about that. He hated them for attacking him and Henry, and for almost killing them. He hated them because he had to live in fear because of them.

That didn't mean he wished they'd died, though. He didn't want anyone to die. He knew it wasn't his fault, and that Alcott and Bay had only been protecting him and Henry. It wasn't an easy thing to wrap his mind around, though.

People had died because of him. They died because they'd attacked him and Henry, and they'd paid the price.

Bay moved closer to him and Henry. "Are you sure you're okay?"

"I will be." Edward swallowed thickly. "How do you get

used to it?" he asked.

"You mean the dead?"

Edward nodded. His throat felt tight. "I know it's not my fault. They were the ones who attacked us, and we weren't even the reason the car exploded. But they died. They wouldn't have if they hadn't been here today."

Bay wrapped an arm around Edward's shoulders and pulled him close. It wasn't quite a hug, but it helped. "It won't be easy for you to get used to the fact that some people died because of what happened. But you're right. It wasn't your fault. They were the ones who decided to attack us. One of them decided to throw a fireball at the car, and it exploded. They wouldn't have died if they hadn't been here, but that was their decision to make, not yours." He hesitated. "You'll probably dream about this tonight, and the nights that will come. I can't say I've been through the same thing, but I have some experience with this. I want you to know that if you need anything during the night, even if it's only reassurance after a nightmare, you can come to me."

Edward was touched, but before he answered, a car drove into the warehouse. It stopped close by, and Dakota jumped out of it, making a beeline for them. "Are the four of you okay?" he asked.

He was frantic, much more than was warranted. Of course, that was probably because Bay and Alcott were more than just bodyguards to him. They were his friends, and he was worried about them, as he should be.

Alcott nodded. "Some burns and debris in my back, but I'll be fine. Pretty sure the same goes for Bay."

Dakota looked at Bay, who nodded. "Nothing's broken, but yeah. We should probably find someone to clean our backs. I'd do it myself, but it's kind of hard considering I can't see anything."

Dakota nodded curtly. "Right. Get into the car. I'll drive

the four of you to the office. I already told the doctors they needed to be on standby for when you arrived. I have to say I'm grateful we can take you to the infirmary rather than to the hospital."

Edward was, too. He didn't want to go to the hospital. He already knew what would happen if they did. The four of them would be separated, and he wouldn't be able to find out what was happening to Bay and Henry. Not that he didn't care about Alcott, but right now, his thoughts were full of the nightmares Bay had warned him about. He couldn't stop thinking about losing Henry and Bay, and it made him feel horrified and lost at the same time.

He jerked when Bay gently pushed him toward the car. "Come on. You might not be in as bad a shape as I am, but you still need a doctor to look you over," he said.

Edward shook his head. "I'm fine."

"You look fine, sure. We still need to make sure that you are, though. It's nothing bad. You do need to see a doctor, though. For my peace of mind. Please."

How could Edward say no to that? "Only if you let a doctor see you, too."

Bay laughed. "I don't think any of you would allow me to say no to that. Besides, I won't deny I'm in pain. That explosion wasn't fun to go through."

Edward moved toward the car, and he almost yelped when something brushed against his fingers. It was only Bay, though, and Edward was stunned when he linked their fingers together. He didn't know what would happen next, but he was sure of one thing—he couldn't stay away from Bay anymore. He'd been trying so hard because he wasn't sure things between them would work, but he didn't think he had a choice, not anymore. Almost losing Bay had made him realize how much he cared for him, and even though it was terrifying to think about a possible relationship between them, the thought of losing Bay was even scarier.

Bay had stuck by Edward's side, and he was glad. The doctors back at the office had tried to shoo him away, but there was no way he was leaving Edward behind. They hadn't insisted because they knew how stubborn he was, and they limited themselves to grumbling. Bay had been relieved. He didn't want to have to fight with anyone.

"Did they tell you anything about Henry?" Edward asked as they left the infirmary.

"They haven't. We're not married or family, so they wouldn't give me any details. But Alcott is with him."

"Don't they know who you are, though? Why wouldn't they tell you?" Edward grumbled.

It made Bay's heart feel too big for his chest. He'd almost lost Edward, and he was still trying to wrap his mind around the fact that he hadn't.

"They might not work in a hospital, but that doesn't mean they don't have rules to follow. He was fine when we left him and Alcott, though. I wouldn't worry, if I were you."

"Of course I worry. He's my brother. If I don't worry about him, who will?"

"Your mother."

Edward rolled his eyes. "She's not here. She's on a cruise, and Henry refused to tell her anything about the letter from Purity. She doesn't know any of this is happening, and frankly, I can't say it was a bad idea. She would have come back if she'd known, and she would be one more person in danger."

And that was the last thing they needed. Bay and Alcott had done their best to keep Edward and Henry safe, but they weren't superheroes. They did what they could, but they'd gotten hurt, and that would make the next few days even more difficult.

When they arrived in the other examination room, Henry was pushing away a nurse and shaking his head at him. "I'm going home," he grumbled.

The nurse put his hands on his hips. "Not as long as the doctor doesn't say you can."

"Do you know who I am?" Henry began, and Bay was relieved when Edward stepped forward.

"Don't be a dick," he said as he walked toward the bed on which his brother was sitting.

Henry's face lit up. "Edward! They wouldn't tell me how you were."

"Same goes for me. Are you okay?"

Bay let the two brothers reunite and turned toward Alcott, who was sitting on another bed, his legs dangling off its side. The doctor was behind him, cleaning his back, and Bay winced. He'd gone through the same thing only minutes ago, and he was grateful it was over.

"Where's Dakota?" he asked.

"He said he was going to his office. I'm ready to bet he's calling in more bodyguards for Edward and Henry. This is even worse than when Benedict was attacked."

Because they'd gotten hurt—it wasn't anything serious, but that didn't change that fact.

Bay wasn't surprised when Dakota came back. He was hovering like a mother hen, and Bay grinned at his best friend. "I'm touched by how worried you are for me, but I'm okay," he said.

Dakota glared at him. "You almost got yourself killed."

"It's not like I did it on purpose. Trust me. I'm not planning to die anytime soon." Not now that he'd finally accepted that he wanted Edward in his life.

Dakota sighed, and his shoulders slumped. "Fine. I know you didn't do it on purpose."

"Do you know what happened? We were headed home, but the driver went to the warehouse instead."

"I talked to him. We found him hiding in a corner of the warehouse. He had the right idea leaving the car. He said that Purity threatened his family, including his newborn daughter."

Bay grimaced. He wasn't happy with the guy, but he could understand why he'd done what he'd done. Besides, he had no doubt that Dakota had already yelled at him more than enough. "We're sure it was Purity?"

Dakota arched a brow. "Who else?"

He wasn't wrong. Still. "We need to be sure."

"We are. They were the ones who approached the driver. He mentioned them by name."

Bay bit his lower lip while he thought. He wasn't sure what Purity thought they would achieve by killing Henry and Edward. Although, maybe they hadn't been trying to kill them. In the beginning, it had looked like they were trying to drag them out of the car, which probably meant they wanted to take them away. Maybe they thought kidnapping them would help stop the deal with Benedict. Bay had no doubt that was the reason why they were doing this.

But now, as far as they knew, both Edward and Henry were dead. That gave Bay an idea.

He looked at Edward and Henry, then back at Dakota. "Purity probably thinks the brothers are dead."

Dakota frowned. "Why?"

"The explosion. Even if several of the attackers managed to save themselves, they can't know what happened in the warehouse after the explosion. That could be to our advantage."

"Explain."

"They're obviously trying to stop the deal between Benedict and Henry. What if we say that Henry died? That way, we would only have to protect Edward. He's the one who would step into his brother's shoes if Henry was dead, right?"

"I don't know. We have to ask them."

Bay wasn't looking forward to that, but it was the only way this could work.

He and Dakota neared the bed, and Edward and Henry stopped talking when they noticed them. Bay hoped Dakota would explain, but instead, Dakota looked expectantly at him.

Bay huffed. "Fine. Coward," he muttered. He turned toward the brothers. "I have an idea."

Edward crossed his arms over his chest. "Something tells me I won't like it."

Bay raised his hands. "It's only an idea, which means that we don't have to do it if we don't feel comfortable with it. I'll follow your lead, of course. But it might help us get to the bottom of this, and it's what we need right now."

"We're listening."

"Purity probably thinks that you and Henry are dead. That would make sense, since they don't know what happened in the warehouse after the explosion. We can't have both of you dying, of course, not if we want to have at least a chance to stop Purity. That means that only one of you has to die. Figuratively, of course."

"We think we should spread the word that Henry died in the explosion," Dakota said.

Bay was so relieved he could have kissed him. "That's what I was trying to say, yes."

"Then I would have to step up and take his place as the CEO," Edward said slowly.

"No. Absolutely not," Henry snapped. "That would put Edward in more danger than he's already in, and I won't accept that."

"The doctor said you needed bed rest," Dakota pointed out.

That was new to Bay, but he wasn't surprised. The four of them were banged up, and if he could get bed rest, he would without hesitation. Unsurprisingly, Henry wasn't okay with that.

"I don't care what the doctor said. I'm going home."

To everyone's surprise, Edward put a hand on his brother's chest and pushed him back down. "Stop it. If the doctor says that you need to be on bed rest, then that's what you're going to do. And don't try to protest, because I don't care. Your ass is staying here, no matter how many times or how loud you yell at me."

Henry blinked at him, then leaned back in the bed. "Fine. But don't you see that you're going to risk a lot? If you step into my shoes and become the CEO, Purity is going to focus on you."

"And can't you see that I don't care? I know what I'm doing, Henry. I might be younger than you, but it's only by five years. I'm not a child. I'm almost thirty, and I've been working for you for years. You know what I can do. You know that even though this scares me, I'm going to do it. I want to protect you as much as you want to protect me. I don't want you to die the next time you're attacked."

Henry shook his head. "I don't want you to become the next target. It was already horrifying enough when I was the target, but if you become the next one, it's going to be even worse. I can't lose you, too. I've already lost Dad and Jessica."

"We'll protect him," Dakota said. "It's going to be easier if we only have one of you to keep an eye on. Alcott will stay with you, because he's in as bad a shape as you are, but Bay will stick with Edward, and I'll assign him more bodyguards. If we're lucky, we might be able to stop Purity entirely."

Henry didn't look convinced. "You really think so?"

"I won't lie to you. I don't think it's going to be easy. But maybe we can get them to back off when it comes to the two of you, and that's my main goal right now."

Henry sighed. "Fine. It's not like I can continue to say no, not when all of you are ganging up on me." He looked at Edward. "But you have to be careful. Promise me."

"Of course I'll be careful."

Henry nodded, then turned his attention to Bay. "And you. If anything happens to my brother, I'll kill you myself. It's a promise, and I'll keep it if I need to."

Bay didn't tell him that if something happened to Edward, he would be more than happy to allow Henry to hurt him. He doubted he would feel anything but pain already anyway.

CHAPTER FIVE

Edward could hear the TV was on in the kitchen, so he stayed where he was in his bedroom. He didn't want to watch the news. The networks had been blasting ever since the attack, saying that Henry was dead, and even though Edward knew it wasn't the truth, it still hurt.

He'd come so close to losing his brother. He didn't know what he would have done without Henry. Some people might think it was weird, but he and Henry were very close. It might be strange because of the age difference, even though five years wasn't a lot, but they'd grown up together. Their father had always been busy with work, and their mother was always busy with her things. She loved to travel and to work with various charities. Often she wasn't alone, either, and Henry and Edward had relied on each other. They still did, in many ways.

Not being able to see Henry, to have him by his side, was weird and hurtful. They would get through this, though. They had to.

He looked at the ceiling of his bedroom. So far, he'd managed to avoid going to the office, but he wouldn't be able to do that much longer. People knew he'd gotten hurt in the attack, but he had new responsibilities, even though Henry wasn't dead. Dakota and Benedict were working on delaying everything so that Henry could step back into his role once he could reveal that he was very much alive, but in the meantime, they needed to put up a good front and get to work.

He'd never wanted anything less than that.

He was worried. Of course, he always worried, so that was nothing new, but this time was different. He didn't know if he would be able to give up the pretense. They hadn't told anyone that Henry was still alive except their mother, and they'd had to text her because she hadn't been answering her phone. It had been a risk, and they hadn't wanted to take any more. Not even Jessica and Lyle, Henry's best friend, knew that Henry wasn't really dead, and Edward wasn't looking forward to talking to either of them.

Edward was also afraid that he would ruin everything. There was more than one reason that he hadn't wanted a place in the family business. He wasn't good when it came to business, not the way Henry was. What if Edward did or said something wrong, and they lost everything? Maybe Henry had been right, and Edward should have faked *his* death. It made more sense now, but it was too late.

Edward huffed and pushed away from his bed. He wasn't going to change anything by moping around, and even though he didn't want to go to the office, it didn't mean he had to stay in bed. He didn't even have to go to the kitchen if he didn't want to watch the news.

He headed outside instead.

He lived in an apartment, so there wasn't much space, but it was enough for him to have a balcony. He kept a lot of plants there because he liked feeling close to the earth. Having an apartment sometimes made him uncomfortable, and being able to sit outside in the middle of his plants was a delight. That was what he did now, sitting in one of the chairs, surrounded by leaves and pots.

He smiled as he trailed his fingertips into the earth from the plant closest to him. He reached out, using one of the roots to scoop up a bit of earth and dump it in front of his feet. He wiggled his still naked toes into it.

Feeling the earth against his skin always made him feel

more peaceful, which was what he needed right now.

He wanted more, so he scooped more earth with both his hands and put it on the ground. Then he played with it.

It came to him as easily as breathing, and he never wanted it to end. He had full control over the earth and roots of the plants around him, and that added to making him feel more peaceful.

He wasn't sure how long he'd been there playing when he heard Bay behind him. They were closer now, even though they hadn't spoken, not really. Bay had given Edward his space because he knew he needed it. Even though Edward knew that his brother wasn't really dead, he still couldn't see him, and the two of them hadn't gone more than a few days without seeing each other since they were kids.

"How are you feeling?" Bay asked.

Edward shrugged without looking at him. "How should I be feeling? I'm fine."

"Are you sure?"

"I wouldn't be saying it if I weren't. Don't worry. I can't say I'm over the moon happy with what's happening, but I'll live."

"I was surprised to see you left your bedroom."

Edward grimaced and finally looked up at Bay. "I'm sorry I've been distant. I've been trying to deal, and it's not easy. I know Henry's alive, but I can't see or talk to him, and I don't like it."

Bay nodded and sat on the floor next to Edward's chair. Edward felt his cheeks heat, but he kept on looking at Bay. He didn't know what he should call the other man. His boyfriend? He didn't know if they were boyfriends. They'd both agreed that they were attracted to each other, but that was the only thing they'd done, even though Edward knew they both wanted more. He never pushed, though. It was one of the reasons Edward was falling even more deeply in love with him, and he knew that eventually, he would have to face his feelings.

He didn't know how he would do that. He wanted more than what they had, too, albeit not in the same sense as Bay did. He wanted to kiss Bay. He wanted Bay to hug him, to wrap himself around him and keep him safe. He wanted intimacy. Hell, he *craved* it. It had been so long, and Edward felt so lonely.

But Edward was still wary and unsure. Even though he knew Bay was a good man and that he would do nothing to hurt him, he couldn't help it. He'd learned to be so careful with his heart that by now, it was instinct. His instinct was working against him when it came to Bay, though. Edward couldn't remember when was the last time that he wanted to give in so much, but something still stopped him.

What was it? He knew Bay wanted to be with him. He also knew that Bay respected who and what he was, and that he wouldn't push. Of course, Edward might still be wrong. He and Bay had spent a lot of time together lately, but it had been mostly for work. They'd gotten to know each other anyway because, well, when two people spent so much time together, it was bound to happen. Edward truly believed Bay was a good man—a man he'd fallen in love with.

But was that enough? What if Bay one day decided that he didn't want to be with Edward anymore? What if he regretted spending time with him?

But what if he didn't?

Edward slightly shook his head at himself and focused back on the earth. He pushed it around with his toes, then used his power to draw in it. At first, it was simple designs— stick figures, a tree, the sun. It brought him back to more carefree times, times in which he and Henry had played around together. He missed that. They were both adults now, and they had their own lives and responsibilities.

And Edward needed to stop thinking as if Henry was dead. He wasn't. He was safe and sound in Dakota's infirmary, no matter how much he bitched that he needed to leave. That wouldn't happen until the doctors gave him the go-ahead, but even then, he would have to go to a safe building until they were ready to reveal that he wasn't dead, however long that took.

It didn't matter to Edward. He might have reservations when it came to faking his brother's death and taking his place, but that didn't mean he wouldn't do it. He wasn't alone. Bay was there to protect him, and that was the only thing he needed.

Bay wanted to do more for Edward, but what could he say that would reassure him? He didn't know if anything would, considering the situation. Edward was worried about his brother, which was entirely understandable. Henry might not be dead, but he was still in the hospital, or rather, in the infirmary that Dakota had set up at the office. It was state-of-the-art, and Henry hadn't been that badly wounded, but Edward still worried.

It wasn't just because Henry was wounded, either. Edward might not talk about it, but Bay knew there was much more to this. Edward didn't like the fact that they were lying to people and that he had to take his brother's place. He'd been hiding in his apartment for the past several days, but they both knew that couldn't last forever.

Bay wanted to do something, *anything*, to help Edward and soothe him. "Henry's safe, you know?" he said.

Edward blinked at him. "Of course. He's still at the infirmary, right?"

"Dakota checked on him a few hours ago. He was fine and making it known to everyone who listened that he wasn't happy about being stuck there."

Edward chuckled. "That's just like him. I'm surprised he allowed this to happen, to be honest. I almost expected him to throw me onto one of the beds and run away then try telling people that *I* was dead. I wouldn't have been surprised if he'd done just that."

But instead, it was the other way around. Edward was the one who had to be in charge right now, and he wasn't used to it. Bay wasn't sure he wanted Edward to get used to it. He knew that Edward liked the quiet and wasn't enjoying having so many responsibilities. He didn't want to be the boss. He wanted to work for his brother, to have a quiet job, to stay in the background. Hopefully, he'd be able to get back to that as soon as Purity was done playing with them.

No one knew what Purity was planning, and Bay was starting to hate the silence. Sure, it was better than attacking them again, but the wait was killing him. He wanted to do something to help Edward get back to his life. Instead, he found himself waiting and wondering what Purity was up to.

They'd attacked because of the deal Henry and Benedict were planning to sign. Even if they hadn't been trying to kill Henry, they at least would have taken him away. But now, they thought he was dead. Would they try to get to Edward, or would they think that he might not sign the deal since his brother was gone? And what would happen when Henry went back to his life? What would Purity do?

Bay and everyone else had a lot of questions, and unfortunately, they didn't have answers. They still had no idea who was behind Purity or what they were aiming for. They still claimed they wanted the elements to stay separated, but it made no more sense than it had in the beginning. After the attack, Bay was sure there was more to this than what Purity was claiming. It was the only way to explain the fact that several elements mixed and attacked them at the same time. If

Purity believed what they were saying, all the people who had attacked them would have belonged to only one element.

And what element would that have been, anyway? Since they had no idea who was behind Purity, they also had no idea which element that person wielded. It could be any of the four, and Bay wanted to know. It would help them in narrowing the suspects, but so far, they had no more information. It was in moments like this that Bay wanted to grab his computer and research, but that wasn't his job right now. His job was to stay with Edward and keep him as comfortable as possible.

Edward tilted his head up to look at Bay again. "I know he's okay," he said. "But I'm afraid I'm going to mess things up. What if I slip up and someone realizes he's alive? What if I ruin everything he and my father have been working for? I know nothing about this. I don't *want* to know anything about it. If I had, then I would have accepted my father's offer to have half the business."

Bay hadn't known that was a possibility, but he wasn't surprised Edward had declined. "You surprise me every day," he murmured.

Edward blinked. "What are you talking about?"

Bay shrugged and decided that he might as well take the risk. He leaned closer, going slow so that Edward could move away if he wanted to. They hadn't talked again about Edward's asexuality, so Bay wasn't sure what Edward's line in the sand was. He didn't know what kind of physical contact Edward wanted or liked, and the last thing he wanted was to hurt Edward. Edward might not want to kiss him, so Bay made sure he had time to move away.

He was fucking relieved when he didn't, though.

Bay kept the kiss light in the beginning, still hesitant. He wanted to touch Edward, to draw him closer, but again, he didn't want to make Edward uncomfortable. Instead, he kept his hands on his thighs as their lips brushed together again and again. He couldn't help but smile. This had to be the best kiss he'd ever given or received, even though it was only a brush of the lips.

Edward leaned back and looked at Bay. "This has been coming for a while," he said.

Bay chuckled. "It has. Both of us have been so distracted that we haven't gotten to it, though."

"And we're not distracted anymore?"

"Sure we are. But maybe this is what we need. A distraction from the distraction."

Edward chuckled and shook his head. "Maybe." He sobered. "But you know I can't have sex with you. I told you about it."

"Who said anything about sex? I certainly didn't."

"I know you believe that you can do this, but it's not as easy as it sounds. Many people have broken up with me because of it."

Bay rubbed the back of his neck. He needed to choose his words carefully. "I've never been with an asexual man. I know a few, but it's not like we discuss what we like in bed or anything like that, and besides, no two people are the same. That means that you might like something one of my friends wouldn't like, stuff like that. But I know that. I know it, and I'm willing to learn." He reached for one of Edward's hands, brought it to his face, and kissed the back of it before releasing it. "And I really like you, Edward."

Edward smiled sweetly. "I really like you, too. I still worry, though. I know sex is important. I might not care about it, but I've been with enough people to know that it *will* become a problem."

Bay couldn't promise him that wouldn't be the case, no matter how much he wanted to. "I don't think sex is that important."

Edward arched a brow, obviously skeptical. "Isn't it?"

"Well, it depends. For some people, it's vital. Some people don't like it at all. Others, like me, can do without. I'm not ruled by my cock, Edward. I'm sure that some days, I'll wish we could have sex, but I'm never going to push you into it. I know you don't like it, and that's okay. Honestly, I'd rather take the intimacy of being with you than having sex if it makes you uncomfortable."

"Intimacy?"

"You know. Well, I don't know if you know. Do you enjoy sharing a bed? And I'm not talking about sex. But you know what one of my favorite things to do is when I have a boy-friend?"

"What?"

"Lying in bed with him when it's raining outside. When we're wrapped around each other listening to the rain, maybe talk a bit, but not an entire conversation, you know? Just a few words here and there, as we rest together and just are. I miss that a lot when I'm single, and I hope to find it with you." Having that would be worth everything to Bay.

Edward couldn't help but wonder if this really could work. He wanted to hope—of course he did—but could he?

That was the crux of the matter, wasn't it? He wanted to believe that Bay was telling him the truth. He wanted what Bay was offering. Still, he couldn't help but wonder if eventually, Bay would resent him for not wanting to have sex with him. Most of the time, Edward forced himself to try it at least once with his partners. It wasn't that he believed a miracle would happen like the people he was with did, but he figured he owed them at least that. He hoped that if they saw that he wasn't kidding, they would understand that his dislike for sex wouldn't change.

It wasn't even a dislike. He didn't hate sex, and he wasn't disgusted by the idea. He just wasn't interested in it, and he didn't see why he should force himself to do it when he didn't want to. Not a lot of people understood, but Bay seemed to, and Edward's chest swelled with hope.

Because yes, even though he wasn't sure he could allow himself to hope, he already was.

He needed to take one more step with that hope in mind. He needed to have faith in Bay and to trust him. He had with his safety and with his life. Why couldn't he trust him with his heart?

He knew why. He wasn't sure he could face another rejection, especially with Henry in hiding and Bay being his bodyguard. He trusted Bay with his life, which was why he didn't want to lose him. That was what would happen if Bay realized he didn't want to be with Edward. Then what would be left? Edward wouldn't have Bay, and he wouldn't have Henry, unless of course, Henry was out of hiding by then.

It felt like an impossible decision to make, and Edward turned his attention back to the earth he'd dug out of the vase. He dragged his fingertips into it, not caring that he was getting himself dirty. He drew another stick figure, and this one looked like Bay, at least in his mind.

After the stick figure, he decided to build a tiny castle. He focused on the small mound of earth, and with his power, he raised it into the air, molding it. It took focus, which meant that in the meantime, he wasn't thinking about Bay.

At least until Bay added water to the mix. Edward wasn't sure where it had come from, since he didn't have water on the balcony, but then, it wasn't the first time he'd seen Bay do something like that. He had when they'd been attacked, too, and it had been impressive. It still was, even though they were in a peaceful situation.

Bay seemed to have realized what Edward was doing, and

he used the water to create a tiny moat around Edward's castle. Some of the earth tumbled into it, and Edward reached out with his power to pull it back up before it got too wet.

His earth and Bay's water should have mixed. They should have acted like they did in nature and created mud.

But they didn't.

Edward's eyes widened as he watched the earth and the water dance together. There was no other word for it. They took on a life of their own, even though they weren't alive, and they twined together, close but not mixing.

That could only mean one thing.

Edward couldn't move. He wasn't sure he could have even if he'd tried, but he was pretty sure that if he did, he would end up flat on his face. He was mesmerized by the dance of the water and the earth, and he couldn't look away. He heard Bay suck in a breath next to him, but neither of them said anything as they watched the elements rise high in the air, continuing their dance and showing both Edward and Bay that they truly belonged together.

They were mates.

Edward opened his mouth to say something, but no sound came out of it. The earth and the water continued their dance until Edward pulled back his power. He could have watched that for the rest of his life, but he knew that he and Bay needed to continue their conversation. He didn't know if them being mates changed anything for Bay, but he felt like his entire world had shifted.

He'd never thought he'd meet his mate, or that he'd realize who they were. It seemed so impossible. He and Bay had discovered they were mates truly because of fate. He was stunned that it hadn't happened when they'd been attacked, but maybe it had, and they just hadn't noticed. It had been a mess of movement, and the explosion hadn't helped.

When Edward pulled back the earth, Bay's water

disappeared. It probably went back to where Bay had taken it from, and Edward waited, not sure he was able to look Bay in the eyes.

What would Bay's reaction to this be? Edward himself wasn't sure how he felt about it. He was happy, of course, but also confused. Bay had told him he wanted to be with him even before they'd realized they were mates, and that was a good thing. Had this changed something, though? They hadn't talked about meeting their mates, and maybe they should have. Edward knew that some people didn't want meaningful relationships with people they weren't destined to be with, and he understood where they came from.

This was different, though. It wasn't like Henry's situation, in which he and the woman he was engaged to had discovered they weren't mates. Edward and Bay were destined to be together, and that would never change.

Everything else had, though.

"So," Bay began. He chuckled.

Edward wondered if he, too, had difficulties thinking right then. "I didn't expect this," he said.

Bay chuckled. "I'm pretty sure no one expected this. That's kind of the point with mates, isn't it? You don't expect to meet your mate. You can't live with the hope that you will because you might never."

"But we did."

"You're right. We did. How do you feel about that?"

Edward wasn't even surprised that Bay was asking that. He was always thinking about others, keeping Edward safe, making sure he was okay. "Confused, I guess. Overwhelmed." He hesitated. He needed to say this, though. "I know we were just deciding if we should try to date and be together, but this doesn't change anything. If you ever want to leave me behind, I'll understand. I know that I'm probably not what you were expecting when you thought about your mate."

"Don't say things like that," Bay snapped. He paused and took a deep breath. "Sorry for snapping. I didn't mean it."

"Of course you did. You wouldn't have otherwise."

"What I mean is that I shouldn't have snapped because you don't deserve it. I understand why you feel the way you do. A lot of people told you that you aren't worth it, that you aren't perfect the way you are, and I hate that. I hate that you believed them. I won't hold that against you, though. It wasn't your fault, and I won't leave you behind. I can promise you that. And it's not just because we're mates. It's because I've been falling in love with you since the first time we met. It's because I want to be with you, and I would want it even if we weren't mates. I don't know what else I can tell you to make you understand that. I'll do whatever I have to do to make you believe me. I'm not going anywhere."

This should be simple. Bay was right. Edward's exes had influenced him, and it was an influence he wished they didn't have. He couldn't do anything about it. He'd tried and tried to ignore the reason they left him behind, but he couldn't, not when it had happened so often.

But Bay wouldn't leave him. He wasn't a bad man. Edward was sure of that, and he trusted him. The fact that they were mates was one more reason to do that.

Even if Bay might have left him behind eventually, he probably wouldn't now that he knew they were destined to be together. Edward didn't want to be a charity case, and he didn't want Bay to feel like he had to be with him, but he knew that Bay didn't do anything he didn't want to. If he was offering this, if he was making promises, it was because he intended to keep them. It should be enough for Edward. It *was* enough for him. The words were hard to say, though—it was almost impossible. He didn't know why, but he needed to get over this. He needed to tell Bay that he wanted him as much as Bay wanted him.

Bay couldn't have been happier. He'd wanted to be with Edward even before this happened, and he hadn't cared whether or not they were mates. He hadn't planned to ask Edward to check. He hadn't wanted to, and after what had happened between Henry and his fiancée, he doubted Edward would have been eager to do it.

But they *were* mates. They knew for sure now, and it changed everything — yet it didn't change anything at all.

Bay still wanted to be with Edward. He still wanted Edward to want him in his life. He had no intention of going anywhere like the dickheads in Edward's past had. He'd felt that way even before, and this only reinforced his knowledge that Edward was perfect for him.

That was what mates were, wasn't it? He'd watched his two best friends find theirs, and they were blissfully happy now. Of course, sometimes they fought and had disagreements, but mostly, they sailed through life with a smile on their faces. He'd been jealous, even though he hadn't said anything. Why should he have? It wasn't their business. He never wanted them to be unhappy because of him.

And now, he'd met his mate, too.

Edward was still hesitant, though. Bay wasn't sure what else he could say or promise to make him see that he wasn't going to betray him, so he stayed silent and gave Edward time to think. It was something Edward often did. When he worked, he liked some alone time to wrap his mind around all the information he had. Bay suspected the same went for this situation, even though it wasn't work.

"I know you promised you wouldn't leave," Edward began.

Even though Bay's instinct was to interrupt him and repeat

that no, he wasn't going anywhere and that the fact that they were mates didn't change that, he kept his mouth shut. He'd already told Edward what he needed to tell him. Repeating the same thing dozens of times wouldn't change that. Now, it was Edward who needed time to think.

"And I believe you," Edward continued.

Bay's heart beat faster in his chest. "You do?"

"I knew you wouldn't leave me even before we realized we were mates. It just wouldn't have been you, and I trust you. I don't know if it's because of the bond or because we got to know each other pretty well since you started protecting me, but I trust my instincts, especially when it comes to you. So yes, I truly believe that you're not going anywhere. But I also know how hard it can be to be with me. That's why I want you to know that I won't hold you to a relationship with me. If you ever realize that it's too much for you, or not enough, I won't push you for more. If you want someone else, maybe someone you just have sex with, we'll find a way to make it work."

Bay had promised himself he'd keep quiet, but he couldn't, not about this. "I am *not* going to find myself a fuck buddy."

"Sex is important, Bay. I might not like it, but I can admit that."

"Sex is important," Bay agreed. "But intimacy is more important. I don't need to have my dick regularly sucked to be okay and to be in love with you. I never want to hear those words from you again. I am *not* going to cheat on you, and that's final."

"It wouldn't be cheating if I agreed to it."

"You shouldn't have to, though." Bay wondered if that was what had happened with one of Edward's previous relationships. Probably. From what he'd heard about the people Edward had been with, he wanted to track them down and strangle them with his bare hands. "Besides, I *don't* want anyone else. You're the only one for me, Edward, and if we are together, that isn't going to change. I promise you that if I ever have a problem, I'll come to you, and we'll talk things out." That was the important part. If they were together, they needed to talk. They couldn't afford to hide anything from the other. That went for all relationships, though, not only theirs.

Edward nodded. "All right."

Bay blinked. After everything, he'd expected to have to work harder to get Edward's approval. "All right?"

Edward smiled. "All right. I was going to say yes to you even before we found out we're mates. It doesn't change anything. It might even make the decision easier because I already trusted you, but this adds a level of protection that I am happy for. I realize I'm insecure, and that's on me. I promise I'll work on it, though."

Bay was almost afraid to do this, but he reached for Edward. "We never talked about what your sexuality means. Do you like to kiss?"

Edward licked his lips. "I do. I like intimacy, just like you were saying before. I wouldn't mind sharing a bed with you and kissing you. I like to cuddle."

"Then you'll be cuddled. I promise you that."

Edward laughed, and he sounded so much freer than he'd been before. That was how Bay knew he was doing the right thing. He knew that Edward's previous relationships had been a mess, and there was nothing he could do about that. But he could be there for Edward, and he could make this relationship as perfect as possible. He was only a man, and he knew he would mess up eventually, but he would try his best not to. And if he did, he would grovel, and he would beg Edward for his forgiveness.

But he didn't want to think about that right now. He didn't want to think about himself failing, because he knew he wouldn't. He'd wanted Edward almost since the first time they'd met, and now, he had him. Edward had agreed to be with him. Bay still wasn't sure what it meant, or rather, what it would mean for his job and for their relationship, but that would come later. They didn't have to figure out every single detail right now, even though Bay felt the need to do just that.

So instead of talking some more, he reached for Edward. He gave him plenty of time and space to move away, but instead, Edward leaned closer, obviously interested in whatever Bay was about to do.

So Bay kissed him.

Right now, he felt like he would be blissfully happy if he could continue to do this for the rest of his life. Edward was so worried about the lack of sex in their relationship, and maybe Bay would eventually, too, but right now, he was in heaven, and he didn't want anything to change.

Edward was it for him. He had been it even before they realized they were mates, and now even more than before, Bay wanted to make him happy. He didn't know if he could do it, but he would try as hard as he could, and he knew Edward would do the same. They were in this together, after all.

Bay was ready to put in the sweat and the time to make this work.

He didn't try to deepen the kiss. Instead, he left that decision to Edward. Edward didn't, either, but they spent a while on the balcony, leaning against each other and kissing, and it was perfect. Bay had never thought about not having sex in his life, but he wouldn't have a problem if it meant he could come home every night to this.

He was getting ahead of himself and of their relationship, though.

After they stopped kissing, they stayed on the balcony for a bit longer. Bay couldn't look away from the small castle Edward had built and that had revealed that they belonged together. He knew he would never forget this moment. He needed to focus on the future, though, and that meant taking care of Edward.

He got to his feet, brushed his ass off, and held a hand out to Edward. "Why don't we go inside? It's almost lunchtime, and you need to eat."

Edward sighed and took Bay's hand. "I suppose we can't stay here forever. I have to go back to work tomorrow."

"You could wait another day or two." Even though it would put a wrench in their plan. Edward didn't have to know that, though. Dakota wouldn't push for him to go along with it, and neither would Bay or Henry. This was hard enough as it was for Edward.

"Are you sure you can do this?" Edward asked as they stepped back inside. His voice was so soft that Bay almost missed the question.

"I can't promise I'll be a hundred percent okay with our relationship for the rest of our lives, but that goes for all relationships, doesn't it? And I won't lie—I want you. I'm attracted to you. I think you're sexy as hell. But you were clear, and I know that's not going to happen, and it's fine with me. I swear I'll tell you if it ever becomes a problem." Bay doubted it would. He could love Edward without ever having sex with him.

That was what he'd been doing since the first time they'd met, after all.

CHAPTER SIX

This wasn't Edward's place. He knew it wasn't, and he felt incredibly uncomfortable sitting in his brother's chair. Still, everyone thought Henry was dead and that this was Edward's rightful place, so he settled down and looked at the office.

He was still uncomfortable.

He sighed. There was nothing he could do about it, so he might as well try to ignore it and focus on what he was supposed to do. He still hated this, though.

"Are you sure you'll be okay?" Bay asked from the door.

Edward forced himself to smile at him. "You'll only be gone ten minutes, right?"

Bay nodded. "Just enough time to check in with security. I promise I'll be back as soon as I can."

"Don't worry about me. I'm safe here."

Bay didn't look convinced, but Edward knew it was because he was worried. They still hadn't heard anything from or about Purity, and Edward was starting to wonder if they ever would. Maybe once he made it clear that even though his brother was gone, he would go ahead with the deal with Benedict. He wasn't looking forward to that, but if it was what it took for them to be able to go back to their lives, then he would.

"Go," Edward told Bay. "I'll scream if anything happens, and people will come running. I'm not alone here, Bay. Even if you're gone for a few minutes, the office is full. I'll be okay."

Besides, Edward and Bay had spent so much time together

since they'd met that Edward needed some time to breathe. Bay would still be in the same building, but he would be on a different floor. It wasn't that Edward wanted time away from Bay, but rather, he wanted to make sure that he could continue living without him.

Their world revolved around each other right now, and while it was always like that when Edward began a relationship, he also knew that he tended to fall too hard, too fast. Bay wouldn't hurt him, not intentionally, so he was different from the other people Edward had been with. Still, a little distance wouldn't hurt them. If anything, it would probably be good for them.

Bay gave Edward one last glance, then he stepped away and left. He left the door open, and it was easier for Edward to relax. No one could see him even with the door open, because the only desk by it belonged to Henry's secretary, and she'd left her desk when they'd arrived.

Edward hated this situation. He hated lying to people and being the reason that they were hurting. He wanted to yell out the truth, but he couldn't.

He turned his attention to the desk so he wouldn't think about it. It was mostly empty, because Henry was a neat freak. Mostly, but not entirely. Edward hadn't noticed it right away, but there was something there — an envelope. And on it, were the block letters he'd seen on only one other envelope

It was a letter from Purity.

Edward looked around, his heart racing in his chest. How had Purity managed to get into the building? Were they watching him even now? It was as if he could feel their gaze on him, and he hated it. He wanted to leave, but he couldn't go anywhere without Bay.

What could he do, though?

He swallowed. What would Henry do in his place? He wouldn't freak out. Edward was sure of that. Instead, he would face the problem head-on, which meant picking up the letter and reading it. It was the last thing he wanted to do, but at least once he knew what was inside, he could call Bay and Dakota and explain.

He took a deep breath and reached for the envelope. He hated that his hands were trembling, but he ignored it as he opened it. He slowly took out a piece of paper, his heart in his throat as he read.

We killed your brother. You'll have the same fate if you don't obey our orders. Abandon the deal with Benedict Hunt, or we'll come for you.

Edward tried to suck in a breath, but he couldn't. His head was swimming with panic. It was the worst thing that could happen right now, and he didn't know what to do.

"Edward? What are you doing here? What's happening?"

Edward had never been so happy to see Lyle, Henry's best friend. "I'm fine," he pushed out.

Lyle stepped into the office. "Are you sure? Because you don't look fine to me."

Edward didn't want him to see the letter. He didn't want anyone to start panicking, but especially not the people Henry cared about. "I'm just nervous and anxious. You know, first day back after everything that happened."

Lyle's expression shifted to sadness. "I should have called you after I got the news that Henry had died. I'm sorry I didn't. I was trying to deal with everything myself."

"It's okay. I understand."

Lyle's gaze fell to the desk. "I don't know what happened, but it's obvious you're freaking out. Why don't we go to the security guys? I'm sure they can help you."

Edward nodded before he could realize what he was doing. Bay was with the security guys. Edward wanted him. He needed to feel safe again, and he knew that would only happen with Bay.

Lyle grinned. "Great. Come on. I'll walk you there."

Edward got to his feet, pushing himself away from the desk. He followed Lyle outside, leaving the letter and everything else behind. He knew Bay would probably want to take him home once he knew what had happened, but he no doubt would come back to the office to take the letter and everything Edward might need, and to look around to check how that letter had gotten there.

Edward wasn't stupid. He might be anxious, and he might be in shock, but he knew that the only reason the letter was there was that someone who worked for Henry had put it on his desk. No one else was allowed in the office.

Henry had been betrayed by someone he trusted, and Edward couldn't deal with that right now. Instead, he let Lyle guide him toward the elevator. When they stepped inside, Lyle turned and pushed the button.

Edward relaxed. He was about to see Bay. He was safe. He probably shouldn't have left and instead should have found one of the bodyguards Dakota had placed in the office, but he was with Lyle, Henry's best friend.

He forced himself to breathe and focused on that. He needed to stop panicking and to be able to explain to Bay and the others what had happened, and that wouldn't be possible if he was freaking out. "Why were you in Henry's office?" he asked Lyle to distract himself.

"I wanted to see you. I heard that you had come in."

Lyle didn't work closely with Edward, but he did work for the company, and Lyle and Henry had been friends since college, which meant that he'd been in Edward's life for a while. He'd probably been worried for Edward, and Edward felt guilty that he was lying to him and that he'd barely thought about him since the attack. "How have you been doing?" he asked.

"I'm okay."

"Henry cared a lot about you." It was so fucking hard to

remember to use the past even though he knew Henry was alive.

Lyle cleared his throat. "I know."

The elevator doors pinged, and Edward stepped outside. He frowned when he realized they were in the parking garage. "Lyle? I think you hit the wrong button." He took a step back to get into the elevator again, but Lyle pushed him forward.

"I'm sorry," Lyle said.

The problem was that he didn't sound sorry and that Edward had no idea what was happening or what Lyle was doing, but it couldn't be good. "Lyle?"

The elevator closed behind them, cutting off Edward's escape.

"I'm sorry things had to come to this, Edward, but I can't miss this opportunity." He reached for his pocket, and Edward was only half surprised to see him take out a gun. "We're going to my car."

Edward swallowed. "And after that?"

Lyle shook his head. His expression was enough for Edward to know he probably would never come back to the office, or see Henry and Bay. "You shouldn't ask questions you don't want the answer to."

"Why?" *That* was a question Edward wanted the answer to.

"Because I was ordered to. Because you're an earth wielder, yet you're in a relationship with your bodyguard, and he wields another element."

Edward didn't bother to ask how Lyle had found out either of those things. "You're with Purity."

"Who do you think put that letter on Henry's desk?"

Bay was smiling as he stepped back into the office. He

couldn't think of it as Edward's office, since Henry would soon be back behind the desk. Besides, the office didn't *feel* like Edward. It was too big, the furniture too sleek.

Bay knew Edward wasn't happy about taking his brother's place, and neither was Henry. Henry was protective, and he didn't want Edward to be in danger. Bay hoped that soon, Henry would be able to come out of hiding, but he wasn't sure that would happen. They still had no idea who was behind Purity, and he doubted they would stop trying to get to the brothers. They had in Benedict's case, but no one knew why, and Bay wasn't willing to risk Edward's life, or Henry's.

He frowned when he saw Edward wasn't behind the desk. He looked around, wondering if maybe he was sitting on one of the couches in the corner, then strode to the bathroom door and knocked. "Edward?"

No answer. Bay frowned even deeper. He went back to the office door, poked his head out, and looked for Henry's secretary. She was there, and she looked up when she heard him. "Do you know where Edward is?"

She shook her head. "I just came back to my desk. I was in the kitchen getting coffee."

"You haven't seen him?"

"No. Sorry."

Bay nodded at her and moved back inside the office. He went to the desk, looking for a hint of where Edward might have gone. His phone was there, which was the second sign that something was wrong. Bay had already been worried, and it was getting worse. He'd told Edward that he needed to keep his phone on him at all times. That way, he could call Bay if he needed to.

Something was wrong. Bay knew better than to do anything on his own, so he called Dakota.

"How is Edward adjusting?" Dakota asked when he answered.

"He's gone."

There was a pause, then Dakota asked, "Gone?"

"I went to talk to the head of security and left Edward in the office. He's not in there anymore, and he left his phone on the desk. I don't know what happened, but I think someone got to him."

"What do you need?"

Bay loved that Dakota didn't doubt him. He didn't ask him if Bay was sure. He just went with it, which was a good thing since Bay was a hundred percent sure that Purity had Edward.

"I don't know. We're mates, Dakota." Bay hadn't told anyone yet. He'd wanted to enjoy that knowledge for a while longer without people asking questions and congratulating him."

"Really?"

Bay felt like he was breaking inside, but he needed to focus and ignore the panic. He could do this. It was his job.

But Edward wasn't just a client. He was Bay's entire life right now, and Bay was terrified that something would happen to him. What if he did the wrong thing? What if he chose the wrong option? He couldn't risk Edward that way, but he knew someone had to do something.

"You're freaking out," Dakota said.

Bay chuckled darkly. "How do you know?"

"I know you. I know how I would feel if I lost Benedict. Breathe, Bay. He might be gone, but it hasn't been for long, which means we can find him."

Bay closed his eyes and obeyed. He breathed in and out, listening to Dakota's breathing on the other side of the phone. When he felt better, he opened his eyes and asked, "Okay. What now?"

"You said his phone is on the desk?"

"It is, so we can't use it to locate him."

"That's not going to be a problem. I expected something like this would happen, so I stuck a GPS into one of his shoes."

Bay blinked. "How did you know what he would wear?"

"I put a GPS in every pair I could find."

Bay could have kissed Dakota, and the only reason he didn't was that Dakota wasn't in front of him. "So you can find him?" If Dakota couldn't, Bay didn't know what he would do.

He didn't want to think about it, not until and unless he had to.

"I can. Wait for me in the parking garage. We can get to Edward together."

Bay wanted to say no. He wanted to go right away. But they had no idea who had taken Edward and how many people Bay would have to face, and he couldn't risk it.

He and Dakota hung up, and Bay snatched Edward's phone from the desk. He put it into his pocket, then headed out. He knew he should call Henry and tell him what was going on, but that was probably the worst thing he could do. Henry would freak out even more than Bay had, and he would leave the safe place where he was hiding to look for Edward. Purity would probably finally manage to get their hands on him, and they would have both brothers. They would have won, and Bay couldn't allow that to happen. Edward wouldn't want it, and neither would Henry if he took the time to think.

So Bay didn't call Henry. Instead, he closed the office door and turned to Henry's secretary, forcing himself to smile at her. "I found him. He got overwhelmed, and he decided to go home."

She smiled sadly. "I understand. Mr. Long wasn't my brother, but I miss him so much. He was a good boss. It's such a pity."

"You're right. I'm going to follow him to his apartment and

check in on him. I hope we'll be back tomorrow, but I'm not making any promises."

"Please, tell him to take a few more days. I know he probably wants to make his brother proud, but he needs time to grieve. We all do, but especially him."

He nodded at her and left. He hated lying, even though it was part of his job. But Henry's personal assistant looked like she really cared, and Bay felt uncomfortable. Henry was alive, and if things went the way they should, he would be back to work soon. Edward would be okay, and he'd be back, too.

He had to be.

Bay needed to believe that. He knew he shouldn't have left Edward alone in the office. He should have insisted that Edward go with him, or have had the head of security come to them. But he'd thought Edward was safe in the office. He hadn't even considered that someone could get to him there.

He looked down at Edward's phone. He knew the passcode to unlock it—he'd had Edward tell him just in case—and he unlocked the screen. He couldn't find any phone calls or texts that would have made Edward leave the office on his own. That meant that the only reason Edward would have left the office was that someone had somehow made him leave. Henry's secretary hadn't been at her desk, but the office was still full of people. Whoever had managed to get to Edward was probably familiar with the place and the people who worked there. Otherwise, they would have been noticed. Hell, they might even be familiar with Edward.

Bay should have known. He shouldn't have left Edward alone, and he would never forgive himself if something happened to his mate. And if Edward died, well, Bay wasn't sure what he would do. Seek revenge, probably. He wasn't suicidal, and he knew Edward wouldn't want him to do that, but he felt guilty. He could only imagine how amplified that emotion would become if Edward was dead.

He couldn't think that way, though. He needed to focus on the fact that Dakota had thought ahead and that he'd put a GPS in Edward's shoe. That meant that they *could* find Edward. It didn't matter that he didn't have his phone with him. Bay would find him soon, and he would bring him home. He would also pound whoever had taken him into the ground. He wouldn't even feel guilty about it. He didn't care who Purity was or what they wanted. They'd touched his mate, and they were going to pay.

Edward had no idea where he was. Lyle had put him into the trunk of his car, so he didn't know how long it was since they'd left the office. He knew Bay had noticed he was gone by now, though. That was the only thing he was sure of, and he hoped Bay was coming after him because he didn't know if he could get out of this alone.

It wasn't his job. It wasn't something he had experience with. He didn't understand why Lyle was doing this, and even if Lyle gave him an explanation, he doubted he ever would.

He pulled on the rope that kept his hands tied to the back of the chair that he was sitting on. Lyle had taken him out of the trunk about ten minutes after he'd parked the car wherever they were. Edward figured it was because he'd come in here to get the chair and the rope ready, and when he'd finally dragged Edward out of the car, he'd pulled him toward the small cabin. Edward wondered if it was Lyle's summer house, but he doubted it could be traced back to Lyle. He might not know why Lyle was doing this, but he was sure his brother's best friend wasn't an idiot.

"You won't get free," Lyle said.

Edward scowled at him. It was the only thing he could do, and he was going to do it, even though it wouldn't help.

"Why are you doing this?" he asked. He was still hoping for an answer, if anything, because Henry would wonder.

If Bay got his hands on Lyle, Lyle wouldn't make it out alive. That meant that Henry would never know why his best friend had tried to kill him and had kidnapped his brother. Of course, Edward would have to survive and tell Henry about it. He wasn't looking forward to that, but he would take that over dying any day.

Lyle leaned against the wall and crossed his arms over his chest. "Why do *you* think I'm doing it?"

"I wouldn't have asked if I knew."

Lyle shook his head. "I thought you were smart, but it's obvious that the brains all went to Henry in your family."

Edward didn't insult Lyle, but it was a close thing. He had to be careful about what he said. Lyle held his life in his hands, and he could snap at any second. "I'm just trying to understand," Edward said, controlling his tone of voice.

"What is there to understand? Can't you see? It wasn't fair."

"Fair?"

Lyle pushed away from the wall and started pacing in front of Edward. "You and your brother don't know what a hard life is like. You were born with everything. You never had to work. You were your father's golden children, and he left the family business to you. But I was there, too. I deserved something. I deserved more than what I got when he died."

Edward blinked. "Wait. You thought my father would put you in his will?" He didn't think he'd ever heard anything so stupid. It was true that Lyle and Henry had been friends for years, although with what Lyle was doing, Edward doubted they'd been that close, even though he'd thought so. But their father had never had anything to do with Lyle. He'd hired him, but that was because Lyle had been a good hire. He'd liked Lyle, but they hadn't been close. He certainly wasn't another son for Edward's father, whatever he seemed to think.

Lyle stopped in front of Edward and smiled. It wasn't a nice smile, and it sent shivers down Edward's back. "He should have. But everything will be mine now."

Edward frowned at that. "Yours?"

"With both you and Henry out of the picture, I'll take over the company."

Edward couldn't stop the snort that escaped him. "Oh, my God. That's why you're doing this? Because you think you're going to inherit the company?"

"I should have killed you first, but I'm sure I'll find a way."

Edward shook his head. "I have a will, and you're not in it. So even if you kill me, you wouldn't get the company. You won't get your hands on it anyway, though, because Henry is alive." Edward knew Dakota and Bay wouldn't allow Lyle to touch Henry. It might be stupid to tell him about Henry, but Lyle didn't know where Henry was. Edward hoped that Bay would realize that he only would have left with someone he knew well and that someone had seen him and Lyle together.

It was a danger to tell Lyle about Henry, because he could go straight to him. He wouldn't find him, though, and Bay, Dakota, and Alcott would protect him. Edward knew that if they had been with him, he would still be in the office, and Lyle would be under arrest. Instead, this was happening to him, and it was his fault for trusting someone he shouldn't have trusted.

"You're lying," Lyle snapped.

"I'm not. After the attack, we decided to fake his death to see what would happen. Purity wanted him gone, and we knew that once it happened, they would focus on me."

"Henry would never allow that. You're his little brother. He would keep you safe."

"He wasn't happy about it, but he agreed to it. My presence

here, or rather, in his office, is proof of that. He faked his death, Lyle. Henry is alive and well, and if something happens to me, he won't stop until he finds out who's responsible."

Lyle shook his head. He was trying hard to look like he didn't care, but Edward knew him. He and Lyle weren't friends, but he'd spent enough time with him to be able to read him. He was starting to panic, and Edward didn't know whether that was a good thing or not.

Before he could say anything else, Lyle punched him in the face.

Okay, so it was a *bad* thing.

It hurt, and Edward wondered if his nose was broken. Lyle wanted to hurt him. He wanted to hear him scream. Edward probably would eventually, but if Lyle wanted that kind of reaction from him, he was going to have to work harder.

Edward wasn't looking forward to the beating, but as long as Lyle was hurting him, he wasn't killing him. The longer Edward managed to stay alive, the more chances there were that someone would find him.

"You're lying," Lyle repeated.

Edward spat out the blood that had filled his mouth, then looked at him. "I'm not. It wasn't easy to convince my brother to do this, but I did. Henry is alive, and he'll come back if something happens to me. You'll never get your hands on the company. It's not yours to take, and you don't deserve it."

This time, Edward wasn't surprised at the punch aimed at his face. He also wasn't surprised that more followed, or that Lyle also started kicking him. He did end up screaming, but he did his best to wait as long as he could.

By the time Lyle was done beating him, everything hurt. The chair to which Edward was tied was on the floor, and the rope around his wrists had loosened. He forced himself to stay still so Lyle didn't notice.

Lyle was panting as he crouched next to Edward and dug his fingers into Edward's hair. He pulled Edward's head back. Edward could barely see him through the blood that covered his eyes and the swelling.

"I wouldn't relax, if I were you. I'll be back soon, and I already have a nice grave dug up for you behind the cabin."

Edward didn't ask why Lyle didn't kill him now. He suspected Lyle wanted to make sure Henry was alive before he hurt him. If Edward had lied, then he would need him to change his will, which meant he had to keep him alive.

Maybe telling him Henry was alive hadn't been a bad thing after all.

Lyle gave Edward one last shake and dropped him back to the floor. Edward whimpered. His body was a ball of pain. He didn't know what hurt more, because *everything* hurt.

He waited until he heard the car drive away to open his eyes. He wasn't sure he could move, but he tried, and after a few tense moments, he managed to free one of his hands.

He forced himself through the pain every movement caused in his body. He had to get out of here. He needed to get back to Bay, to find a phone, something that would enable him to contact his mate. He didn't know if he was about to die because of the injuries or how long he had until Lyle returned, but he had to let Bay know that Lyle was the bad guy.

Lyle hadn't said he worked for Purity, but Henry wouldn't care. Whatever the reason Lyle had done this, Henry would have his head once he found out.

Of course, for him to find out, Edward needed to get out of here.

It took what felt like an eternity to get himself out of the chair. Once that was done, Edward dragged himself toward the door. He didn't have his phone, so he would need to find another way to contact Bay. At least Lyle wouldn't get to Henry. No one but Dakota and Alcott knew where he was, and he didn't have his phone with him, either.

Even if Edward died today, his brother would be safe.

It took almost as long, or maybe longer, for Edward to half drag himself, half walk, to the main road. His entire body was on fire by the time he got there, and he wasn't sure he could take one more step or drag himself another inch forward. And now that he was here, he didn't know what he was supposed to do. He tried to stay on his feet, but his knees wouldn't hold him up. They buckled, and he fell.

He pressed his forehead to the ground and closed his eyes. He could feel the wind on his skin, and oddly, on one of his feet. He was cold, and the world around him was getting darker, even though he knew it shouldn't be. It wasn't that late yet.

Then a loud sound made Edward jerk. He forced his eyes open again and watched the car coming closer. He prayed it wasn't Lyle coming back to finish him. He wouldn't have the strength to keep Lyle away, and he knew that if it *was* Lyle, he wouldn't be alive for much longer.

He'd fought. He'd done his best to get out of this situation. But he was too tired to continue to fight, so he closed his eyes and prayed that if it was Lyle, he would make Edward's death a fast one.

Bay was itching to do something. Dakota had told him to wait in the parking garage, but he couldn't stay still, so he was pacing by his car, waiting for his boss to get there. It felt like an eternity had passed, but Dakota still wasn't here.

Bay had to do something. He wanted to go find Edward. He wanted to get his hands on whoever had taken Edward from him and hurt them. The only problem was that the only way he had to find Edward was through Dakota, who still wasn't there.

A car drove toward Bay, going too fast, and he found himself hoping even though he didn't recognize it. When the man who was driving hopped out after parking, Bay's shoulders slumped. It wasn't Dakota. He'd known it, but seeing it made it worse.

He did know this man, though. They'd never talked, but this was Lyle, Henry's best friend, and he worked for the company. His presence here wasn't a surprise, but something about it made Bay frown, even though he couldn't quite put his finger on what it was. Lyle looked flustered, and when he saw Bay standing there, he took a step back as if he expected Bay to hit him. Bay didn't like being feared, so he forced himself to smile even though he felt like he was dying inside. "Lyle, right?" he asked.

"Yes. Who are you?"

"Edward's bodyguard."

Lyle's eyes widened, and he looked around.

The movement felt fake, and Bay's instinct rose.

"Where's Edward? Since you're his bodyguard, I assume he's here, too?"

"He will be." Bay wasn't about to tell Lyle that Edward was gone, especially not if Lyle was hiding something. Bay couldn't be sure, of course, but his instincts didn't usually steer him wrong. He didn't know if whatever was up with Lyle had to do with Edward, but he couldn't risk it.

He stepped closer, and he wasn't surprised when Lyle moved back again. "Do you know where Edward is?" he asked, doing his best to keep his voice calm.

Lyle shook his head frantically. "Of course not. Why would I know where he is?"

"You tell me."

"I have nothing to tell you. I just arrived. I don't know what happened, and I don't care."

"You work here, don't you?"

Lyle blinked and nodded. "I do."

"Why are you so late?"

"I was busy. Neither Henry nor Edward hold me to normal work hours."

Henry. Lyle was his best friend, and even though Bay had never seen them together, he expected a best friend to feel strongly about Henry's death. Lyle didn't give him that impression, though. He was nervous, and it was obvious he was expecting something to happen, but he didn't look sad. "Henry?"

Lyle shrugged. "He's my best friend."

"You mean *was*, right?"

Something passed in Lyle's eyes, and now Bay was sure he had something to do with this. He didn't have time to coax information out of him, though, so he moved even closer until Lyle's back hit the wall. Then Bay reached for him, bunching Lyle's shirt with his fist and pulling him closer until their faces were only inches away from each other.

"What did you do to Edward?" he asked.

Lyle seemed to realize that if he didn't give the right answer, Bay wouldn't let him walk out of this place on his feet. He might be able to drag himself if he was lucky. He shook his head. "Nothing."

"I don't believe you."

"I don't know Edward that well. I'm Henry's best friend, not Edward's."

"What do you know about Henry, then?"

Bay knew he was right about Lyle being involved when Lyle's gaze shifted to the side. "Nothing. He's dead."

"He is. Edward isn't, though, and he's missing. I want to know what you did to him."

"I told you I didn't do anything."

"And I don't believe you." He leaned even closer and let Lyle feel his breath on his face. "I might be Edward's bodyguard, but it's not the only thing I am to him. I love him, and I'll find him, with or without your help. It would be better for you if you talked, though." This way, Bay wouldn't have to wait for Dakota to arrive.

"I don't know—"

"Don't say that you don't know what I'm talking about because it would be a lie." Bay slammed Lyle against the wall, and he grinned at the satisfying sound of Lyle's skull hitting the cement. "It hurts, doesn't it?" he asked.

Lyle's eyes were filling with tears. "You're a savage. How can you do this to me? I'll—"

Bay slammed him against the wall again, then a third time, just to make sure that Lyle understood what was happening. "I don't care what you'll do. I want to know where Edward is, and I know that you know. Tell me, and I might let you live."

Bay couldn't help but wonder why Lyle had taken Edward. He was sure that was what had happened, but he still didn't know where Edward was. It didn't make sense, though. Lyle was Henry's best friend. Why would he kidnap Edward?

Maybe he would if he worked with Purity. Bay didn't know who worked with them, but it was obvious that they had a lot of people in the cult—or whatever they were. Lyle could be one of them. Since he thought Henry was dead, he'd turned his and Purity's attention to Edward. Bay didn't like it, but he had to face the reality that even though Lyle was Henry's friend, he was part of Purity, that he'd taken Edward, and that he might have killed him.

"You can't do this," Lyle said.

"I can do whatever I want."

"I'll have you arrested. I'll make sure that you never see the light of day again."

Bay grinned. "That's only going to happen if I let you live."

Lyle's eyes widened. "All right. I'll tell you everything as long as you don't hurt me."

"Good boy." Bay allowed Lyle to slide down the wall until his feet touched the ground. He stayed close, because he didn't trust Lyle as far as he could throw him, and he wasn't surprised when Lyle tried to push around him.

Bay grabbed him again and slammed him against the wall one more time. He waited until Lyle could breathe again, then said, "I'm waiting."

The sound of a car coming close made both of them look back, and Bay prayed Lyle would speak before it got to them.

"Purity took him," Lyle said. He straightened his back and looked straight at Bay. "What he and his brother were trying to do it wasn't right. We shouldn't mix."

Bay rolled his eyes. "Spare me. I don't care what you think. I just want to know where Edward is. And I hope for your sake that he's alive and well, because if you touched one hair on his head, you'll regret it."

The car stopped, and Dakota hopped out of it, making a beeline for Bay. Bay made a disgusted sound and let go of Lyle, who rushed toward Dakota. "Please. He attacked me. Call the police."

Bay rolled his eyes again, then asked, "You have the coordinates?"

Dakota nodded and wiggled his fingers. "Give me your phone. I'll enter them." He looked at Lyle. "I'll take care of the trash once you're gone. You'll have to tell me what happened, though."

Bay handed his phone to Dakota and tilted his chin at Lyle. "Not sure yet, but he has something to do with Edward's disappearance, and probably with the attack, too. Don't let him leave."

Bay wanted to see what would happen next, but as soon as Dakota was done with his phone, he headed out, using the coordinates to get to Edward. He drove too fast, but he didn't care. No one tried to stop him, which was a good thing because he was pretty sure he would have knocked out anyone who had.

When Bay got to the place the coordinates indicated—a wooden cabin in the middle of nowhere—it was afternoon. The trees around the cabin made everything look dark, though. Bay ignored the churning in his stomach and rushed inside, his heart feeling like it fell down to his stomach when he saw the chair on the floor and the blood. Edward had been tied there at one point.

But he wasn't anymore.

It didn't take long for Bay to look through the cabin, but it was empty. Once he was done, he rushed outside and looked around.

Edward was nowhere to be found, but Bay understood why the coordinates had brought him here when he found one of Edward's shoes on the path to the main road.

He picked it up and raked a hand through his hair. What was he supposed to do now? He could call Dakota, but since he suspected that the GPS was in the shoe he was holding, it wouldn't help. Still, maybe Dakota had managed to get something out of Lyle, so Bay took his phone out of his pocket.

It rang before he could do anything. He answered, hoping he was Dakota, but instead, Edward's voice greeted him. "Bay?"

He sounded weak, but Bay's knees buckled with relief. Edward was alive. "Edward. Where are you?"

"The hospital."

"I'm coming. Just tell me which hospital." And once he was there, Bay was never letting Edward out of his sight again. He couldn't go through this a second time. It would kill him—or he'd kill whoever would be responsible for it.

CHAPTER SEVEN

Edward felt like shit. His entire body hurt, and he wasn't sure how he'd gotten to the hospital. One of the nurses had told him that a car had found him by the side of the road and had driven him there. He was grateful, and he wished whoever had found him had stuck around so he could thank them. The nurse had also warned him that they'd had to call the police, and that eventually, he would need to answer questions.

Right now, resting was the only thing he had the strength to do.

He was stretched out on the bed, his entire body on fire. The nurse had wanted to give him a painkiller, but instead, he'd asked for her phone. He knew that whatever painkiller was given to him would probably knock him out, and while he no doubt needed some sleep and rest, he wanted to see Bay first. He was grateful that the nurse had allowed him to use her phone to call Bay. He wanted Bay here when the police arrived.

Whoever was behind Purity, they had a lot of power, and no doubt a lot of money. Edward suspected that even if the police arrested Lyle, he'd be out before Edward left the hospital. Either that or he'd be dead, because Purity didn't strike Edward as forgiving.

Right now, he wouldn't mind that second option.

He closed his eyes against the harsh light of the hospital room. He wanted Bay, but he didn't know how long it would take him to get here. He wasn't even sure which hospital he was in. The nurse had mentioned it when she'd called Bay, but Edward couldn't remember. He probably should ask, but he didn't have the energy to do more than just lie there and wait. He was lucky the nurse had taken pity on him and given Bay instructions, including Edward's room number.

Edward opened his eyes when he heard the door open, and even though smiling hurt, he did. Bay stepped in, his gaze stopping on Edward. Then he rushed to the bed, tripping and almost falling on his face in his haste and took one of Edward's hands.

Edward winced. Bay noticed it, of course, and he let go. Then he hovered over him, looking like he wanted to drag Edward into his arms, but knowing it would hurt him. "What happened to you?" he asked softly.

"Lyle. Henry's best friend. He's what happened to me." Edward tried to sit up, but Bay gently pushed him back down. Edward shook his head. "You have to find him. Please. I told him that Henry was alive, and I'm scared that he's going to hurt him."

"I already stopped him. He came back to the office, and I was waiting for Dakota in the parking garage. I knew something was up with him by the way he behaved, and I left Dakota with him. He's not going anywhere, Edward. Don't worry."

Edward allowed himself to relax. He'd half expected Lyle to come back and try to kill him, or worse, to find Henry. He knew that would be impossible, but fear wasn't rational.

"Can you tell me what happened?" Bay asked.

Edward licked his lips. "I was an idiot. I followed him. I wasn't feeling great, and he found me in Henry's office. He told me he would walk me to the security room so I could be with you, and I agreed. I trusted him. He's Henry's best friend, and he's always been in my life."

"It makes sense. Why shouldn't you trust him?"

"You told me not to move from the office, and I should

have obeyed. Instead, this happened," he said, gesturing at his hurting body. Even that movement hurt.

"Don't think that way. It was a mistake, but you'll be okay. What did he do to you?"

"He beat me. I think he believed that with Henry and me gone, he would inherit the company. I don't know why, and I told him that even if we were both dead, the company wouldn't go to him. I also told him that Henry was alive." Edward sucked in a breath. "I need to go to Henry."

"Don't worry about that. I called Alcott on my way here. Since Lyle is still with Dakota and won't hurt anyone else, Alcott is bringing Henry here."

"Thank you." Edward wasn't sure what he would do without Bay or Dakota. Probably feel lost. Hell, if Bay hadn't been in his life, he might still be in that cabin, waiting to die. It was kind of ridiculous, but he couldn't deny that a big part of what had given him the strength to drag himself out of the cabin was knowing that Bay was waiting for him.

Edward hadn't known if he and Bay could have a relationship, and he still didn't. He wanted to try, though. He'd kept himself away from people for so long that he wasn't sure he knew how relationships worked anymore, but Bay wasn't just a guy. He was Edward's mate, and Edward knew they could make things work. He was going to do his best. He'd almost died, and what would he have been remembered for? Who but Henry and their mother would have missed him?

Edward didn't want to think about dying anymore. He was safe, and if he had anything to say about it, he would never put himself in that kind of situation again.

The door slammed open, making Edward jerk. He grimaced at the pain, but then Henry was on him, climbing onto the bed to hug him. Edward whimpered and tried to push his brother away, but thankfully, Bay was there.

"Give him space to breathe," he told Henry, gently pulling

him back. "He's wounded. You're making him feel even more pain by dragging him around like that."

Henry jerked back. "God, Edward. I'm so sorry."

Edward shook his head. "Don't be. I'm happy to see you, too." He'd thought he would never see his brother and Bay again, and he was so relieved that he wanted to cry.

Henry sat on the edge of the mattress while Bay and Alcott hovered close by. "I can't believe Lyle did this."

"He was jealous."

"I should have known."

"How could you have? He's your best friend. You didn't think he could do something like this."

"Still."

"Stop blaming yourself," he said, trying to keep his voice hard but doubting he would actually manage. He felt weak, much more than he could remember ever feeling. "It was his decision. He decided to kidnap me and to beat me. You had nothing to do with it."

"I wanted to tell him I was okay. I asked Dakota about it, and I got angry when he told me that it was better not to tell anyone, not even my best friend."

Edward could only imagine what would have happened if Henry had told Lyle about this, and he was glad he hadn't. "Stop that," he told his brother. "I'm fine. In pain, but I'll be okay." He reached for Bay, and Bay barely hesitated. He linked their fingers together and gently cradled Edward's hand in his.

Henry's eyes widened. "What's going on?" he asked.

"I wanted to tell you, but I couldn't contact you. We're mates." Edward prayed that Henry wouldn't be sad after what had happened with Jessica, but he shouldn't have worried. A smile curled Henry's lips, and he reached out and gently hugged Edward. "I'm happy for you. You deserve happiness, and I know Bay will give that to you," he murmured in

Edward's ear.

Edward looked at Bay. "I know. I'm happier than I've ever been."

Henry snorted as he leaned back. "You're lying in a hospital bed."

"Doesn't change the fact that I'm happy." Because Edward had something that he'd never thought he would have. He had a mate and a relationship. He had his brother, and hopefully, they were both safe now.

"Did he only do this because he wanted the family business?" Henry asked.

Edward didn't know, so he looked at Bay, who shrugged. "I think it's a mix of the two," he said. "From what he told Edward, that was his main goal. He never mentioned Purity, but he did say that what the two of you are doing wasn't right and that the elements should be separated. I wouldn't be surprised if Purity realized how he felt about you and the company and tried to use him to get to you."

"Do I have to go back into hiding?"

"I don't know. We're pretty sure that Lyle contacted whoever his boss at Purity was after he left Edward behind and told him that you were alive. It's no use for you to keep on hiding. I think you should go back to your life, but we'll have to talk to Dakota about that first."

Henry nodded. He looked relieved, and Edward was happy for him, even though he was also worried. He didn't know what would happen next. Purity wasn't done with them by a long shot, and it was terrifying.

But he wasn't alone facing this. He had his brother and Bay. He had Dakota and Alcott, and even Benedict Hunt. Together, they could do this.

Or at least, Edward hoped so.

YOU MAY ALSO ENJOY THE FOLLOWING FROM eXTASY BOOKS INC:

Rocco
Catherine Lievens

Being the doctor for the council assassins was a strange job. Some days, Rocco and the twins were crazy busy. When one of the assassins was wounded, they needed to focus on him or her, and that usually meant long hours. Most of the time, though, their job consisted of hanging around waiting and cleaning the infirmary. On the one hand, it was a good thing since it meant that the assassins were good at their jobs and healthy, but on the other, it was kind of boring. Of course, things were different now that Cam was in the infirmary. Still, having a doctor and two Nix taking care of him was a bit too much. There was nothing they could do twenty-four-seven, which was why Rocco was usually the one sticking with Cam.

But the twins needed something to do, which was why they were cleaning the infirmary right now. They were used to it, and Rocco couldn't help but smile at the banter between them. He'd worked with them for a few years, even though he'd been the assassins' doctor for longer than that, and he was grateful for their presence. Things had been hard when he'd been working alone. Rocco hadn't had access to a Nix who could heal the assassins, and he needed to do everything on his own. It meant that whoever got wounded back then was out of commission for a while. Now, it mostly wasn't a problem. Unless someone was badly wounded, they were usually back to work in a few days.

Cam was different, though. Not only he wasn't an assassin, but it would take him much longer than a week to heal. Rocco kind of wanted to wrap him in cotton and make sure that nothing else could hurt him, and he wanted to keep everyone away from him because he knew how uncomfortable Cam was with people, but he was also aware of the fact that Cam needed this. He needed people hanging around. He needed to have as normal a life as he could considering everything. It wasn't easy after the time he'd spent in the lab, but having the twins around probably helped, even though Cam barely talked to them most days. The twins didn't mind. They might not be assassins, but they'd been through a lot too, and they understood where Cam was coming from. They'd had more time to heal, and they knew how hard his recovery would be. That was why they weren't pushing, and Rocco wasn't, either.

The infirmary door slammed open, making all of them jump. Rocco's attention went straight to Cam, who was trying to scramble up the bed to press his back against the wall. He didn't need to, but of course, he was acting on instinct.

Rocco ignored whoever had entered and went to his mate. "Relax. It's just a patient," he murmured.

Cam turned wide eyes toward him. "How do you know that?"

They both looked at the door at the same time. Rocco groaned when he saw what was waiting for him. "What happened this time?" he asked.

He gently patted Cam's thigh, then went to Julian, who was cradling his arm against his body. Roark was standing behind him, looking sheepish as he rubbed the back of his neck. "I might have gone overboard," he said.

Julian scowled at him. "Overboard? You broke my arm!"

Roark rolled his eyes. This wasn't the first time Julian ended up in the infirmary, and it was always for the same reason. He wanted to be a council assassin, but the problem was that all the assassins had something more. They'd been in labs, and they'd been modified. Roark had the power to enter people's minds and make them believe they were in other places. Julian, on the other hand, was just a shifter. He was good at his job, or at least that was what Rocco had been told, but he couldn't compare.

That was also why Julian had been jealous of Roark, and why he'd tried to get to him several times. Rocco still didn't know if he'd been planning to kill Roark, but knowing Julian now, he doubted it. Still, Julian was in trouble, and he was running from someone. That was why he was living with the assassins. It couldn't be easy for him considering how free he'd been before and how stuck he was in the house now, but he never complained.

Instead, he trained with the assassins, which often ended in him getting hurt.

Rocco gestured at the bed closer to the door. "Sit down."

Julian started to salute but winced in pain. "Got it, Doc," he said instead.

If it really was a broken arm, it would be easy enough to heal him. Rocco looked at the twins, but to his surprise, Tali was doing a good job ignoring him and looking away. It made Rocco frown, but he didn't have the time to check what was happening. "Jolyn? Do you want to come here and heal Julian?"

Jolyn looked at his brother, then back at Rocco, and nodded. "Sure. Give me a few seconds to wash my hands. I'll be right there."

"He's not going anywhere anyway."

Julian groaned. "How do you know that? Maybe I'm planning to run away."

Rocco rolled his eyes — again. "You want to run away with a broken arm? Be my guest. You're giving me more work than all the assassins put together these days, so I wouldn't object."

"It's not my fault Roark is a brute."

"You wanted to train," Roark cried out.

"To train, yes. Not to get my arm broken."

"You insisted I use my power."

"I didn't expect you to attack me while I was distracted. Why did you make me see that I was in the forest and then attacked me only seconds later? You could at least have given me some time to get used to what I was seeing."

"I never gave time to my marks."

"I'm not a mark."

"Yet."

Rocco smiled. Those two were always at each other's throat, but it was evident that they were friends. It was a good thing. Julian had to feel a bit odd being in the house with all of them. He wasn't a mate, but he also wasn't an assassin. He didn't belong to either group, and he'd only recently moved in.

Julian turned his attention to Rocco. "I'm sorry I'm giving you so much work."

Rocco shrugged. "It's fine. At least my life isn't boring."

Julian's eyes glittered. "Right, because you only work when someone is wounded." His gaze quickly went to Cam, but it didn't linger there. "What do you do when you're not working?"

Rocco blinked. "What do you mean?"

"Exactly what I said. What do you do when there's no one in the infirmary to take care of? And how did you become the doctor for the assassins? Have you always been a doctor, or is this a second job? And who have you healed more often? Please, tell me it's Roark."

Rocco shook his head and ignored the steady stream of words coming out of Julian's mouth. As soon as Jolyn got back, they went to work on Julian. Rocco also ignored the winces and groans and the way Julian kept wiggling, and he and Jolyn patched him up.

Julian never stopped talking, and Rocco wasn't surprised. He seemed to have an endless list of topics to ask about. He had to breathe every few so often, though, and Rocco took advantage in one of those moments to gently push Julian toward the door, where Roark was waiting. "You're all patched up. There's nothing else we can do."

Julian blinked and looked down at his arm. "Already?"

Rocco felt the need to roll his eyes yet again, but he was pretty sure that if he continued, they would eventually fall off his face. "Be careful for a few days. The bone is healed, but it's still fragile and sensitive. Take it easy, make sure you don't get into another fight, and for the love of God, don't train."

This time, Julian did salute Rocco. "Got it, Doc. Do you need to see me again?"

"Please don't come back. You never stop talking."

Julian grinned. "It's part of my charm."

Rocco wasn't sure whether or not Julian was flirting with him, but it didn't matter. He pointed at the door. "You can go. Now." Rocco would go crazy if he didn't.

ABOUT THE AUTHOR

Catherine is the creator of several series, most of them paranormal, including the Whitedell Pride Series and the Gillham Pack Series. While she graduated in translation, she decided to go the writer's way because it was more fun to create her own stories and characters.

She's been living in Italy for more than twenty years, but she's a daughter of the North—Belgium to be precise—and she misses it so much that she's already planning to move back.

She loves pizza—probably too much—her son, her pets, and of course, books. She sneaks some reading time into her schedule every time she has five minutes free from writing, demands from her various pets and son, and lastly, housework.

Connect with her:

lievens.catherine@gmail.com
BookBub: https://www.bookbub.com/authors/catherine-lievens
Website: https://authorcatherinelievens.com/
Facebook: https://www.facebook.com/catherine.lievens.9
Facebook Group: https://www.facebook.com/groups/411788002341528/
Twitter: https://twitter.com/authorCLievens
Newsletter: http://eepurl.com/c-uvKn

www.ingramcontent.com/pod-product-compliance
Lightning Source LLC
Chambersburg PA
CBHW060629130626
46555CB00002B/727